THE VAMPIRE PRINCE

Beyond The Mist

VALERIE TWOMBLY

Copyright © 2021 by Valerie Twombly

Edited by JRT Editing

All rights reserved.

No part of this book may be reproduced in any form or by any electronic or mechanical means, including information storage and retrieval systems, without written permission from the author, except for the use of brief quotations in a book review.

Print ISBN: 978-1-7923-6470-9

❦ Created with Vellum

INTRODUCTION

A vampire prince

Lucien has a dark secret, and he will give up his soul to keep it from being discovered. When the mate he has waited centuries for finally reveals herself, he is torn. He's tired of being alone, but claiming her threatens more than the unveiling of his secret. Thousands of lives are at stake.

A rebel fae

As a personal guard to her king, Elaina isn't afraid of much except the vampires. They slaughtered many of her kind, and even though that was centuries ago, she's struggling to trust. One dark prince sets her on edge. Her body is drawn to him, but her mind knows he is hiding something and she is determined to find out what.

The future beckons

The day has come when Lucien must face his past and choose his future. Elaina's visions show two roads. One leads to destruction and

INTRODUCTION

the other to salvation. The choice the fated couple makes will determine the outcome for not only themselves, but for their entire race. The problem is, they have no idea which is the correct one.

CHAPTER 1

Lucien leaned against the stone pillar, his gaze glued to her. She was fluid in her motions, yet lethal as she trained with another fae in the expanse of grass outside the palace. He could appreciate why King Trevan had chosen Elaina as his royal guard. Her fae magic sparked the air with a current that reached all the way to where he stood. His skin prickled and he couldn't stop the smirk that turned up the corner of his mouth. He had to wonder if she had intentionally sent the spark his way.

She despised what he was.

It was all Elaina could do to be civil to him while they worked in Glenmoore assisting Storm with the new fae territory. He couldn't blame her, really. He was born of evil. A blood-drinking predator that was all hardness while she was a soft beauty that was a miracle of nature. His ancestors had killed hers. Drank from them until they had been nothing but bags of bones. His fangs ached and threatened to expose themselves to the fact that he wondered what she tasted like.

Would her magic slide across his tongue?

Would she soften against him and moan in pleasure?

He cursed. Not only did his fangs ache, now his dick was rock hard. He shifted his weight and moved his gaze to the other fae that Elaina was busy training. Or beating the ever-loving shit out of. Depended on how you looked at it. It didn't help because he found his gaze moving back to her once more. A prick of jealous rage ignited inside him that another man dared touch her, even if it was in that man's own self-defense. Lucien's mind wandered further down the rabbit hole and to the fact that he knew Elaina had also been fucking King Trevan. He'd smelled the fae king on her when he'd been in Drudora to search for his missing friend, Roman. That entire mission had started as a clusterfuck that had eventually turned into a history-making event.

Roman, royal guard to Lucien's brother Andrei, had been in Drudora. A fae territory off limits to them because of an ancient war between long-dead brothers. Roman had been fated to King Trevan's daughter, who was a half mortal, half fae female, and while visiting the fae king, Roman had gone missing. In the end, things had turned out for the better. Everyone learned that Storm, the fae princess who had been living in Hetus with the vampires, was not Trevan's long-lost cousin but his very own sister. Both she and Trevan worked together to open the borders between the war-torn territories of Drudora and Hetus. As part of the celebration, Trevan had gifted his sister with her own territory of Glenmoore, thrown a royal wedding for his daughter and her fated, and everyone was one big fucking happy family now.

Except for Lucien.

It started right after Roman discovered Harper was his mate. The dreams. Lucien had dreamed of his own mate, as was normal for his species. She had come to him as a faceless female, so he had figured she had just been born. Not yet old enough to take part in the sexual energy the nightly dream escapades would bring. How wrong he had been. While it should fill him with joy, instead his gut was twisted in a knot. He knew his mate to be of age and was certain she had lost no sleep thinking of him. Unless it was to plot how to drive a stake through his heart.

"You look annoyed. Did someone piss on your boots?" The silky voice jerked him to attention, and he stared into ice-blue eyes. Eyes that could never hide the intense distrust of him. Unable to stop, his gaze roamed downward to the form-fitting black tank and leggings she wore before he looked back into her icy stare.

She tilted her blonde head. "I wonder, can you be trained to like the taste of normalcy instead of sinking those disgusting fangs of yours into someone's flesh?" She leaned closer. So close he could crush her to him and take what he wanted, except she would lash out with her magic and he would have to pretend to be defenseless against her. She wasn't a normal fae. Then again, he wasn't a normal vampire either. Elaina was descended from a powerful line of magical creatures, and he from... Well, he was a dark, dirty secret.

"Does the blood on my hands entice you?"

He looked down. It wasn't *that* blood he wanted. It was hers and controlling himself was becoming difficult. He rolled his fingers into his palms and squeezed. He dared not speak because that would reveal that he had no control around her. Instead, he met her defiant gaze once more.

"Soon our work here will be complete, and I can go home. It cannot happen quick enough for me." She moved away from him when his temper reached critical, and he grabbed her wrist.

"In a hurry to go back to fucking your king?" He just couldn't leave that one alone.

Her gaze zeroed in on him and shot daggers of disgust. "Who I fuck is none of your business." She sent a zap of her power to his fingers, causing him to release her. Then she stormed away.

"Oh but it is my business, dragâ mea. You are mine and I will claim you if I have to kill the fae king to do it," he whispered.

ELAINA STORMED AWAY, HER MOOD NOW FOUL FROM HER ENCOUNTER with the vampire. She had only been in Glenmoore for a few weeks, helping Storm with the new fae territory at the urging of her king, Trevan. It pleased her all the fae were free of the war their predecessors had started so long ago that many of the youngsters had no idea why their world was split. The vampires caused her concern. Especially Lucien, who looked at her like he wanted to devour her.

She shivered.

It was well known to her that his ancestors had killed her people.

The war between brothers, over a female who was Elaina's grandmother, had taken place two millennia ago. Brother Micah had fled with Nina and created the territory known today as Hetus. Jarrah, who ruled over Drudora, retaliated by creating a species of blood-sucking demons he called vampires and set them upon Hetus to destroy his brother and the fae who had dared commit treason against him. Besides her grandmother, there had been other family members who had gone to Hetus and perished at the fangs of Lucien's ancestors. If stories were to be believed, Lucien was not one of the original vampires like his friend Roman but born from the union of a male vampire and his mate.

Micah had used his powerful magic to alter the vampire's DNA. A few, like Roman, had been a blood-sucking demon one day and a so-called civilized vampire the next, while others evolved by birth. It was her understanding that the vampire king—Lucien's brother Andrei—had been one of those born.

She stopped in her tracks. Angry that her body reacted to the vampire prince in such a manner that caused her to desire his touch. All while her mind was filled with disgust at herself and all the reasons this was bad. So very, very bad. There was something else that bothered her. The true origin of the vampire royalty and the other born vampires. Things simply didn't add up to her.

She did a quick memory search of the conversation she had with her sister, Cassia, before Elaina had executed her for treason against the crown.

"Sister, why?"

Cassia had glared at her from her prison cell. "You know nothing about our past, do you? Grandmother gave us the key to control the vampires and I would have had this one except for his mating instinct was far greater than his urge to kill."

"What are you talking about?" Elaina pressed. She needed to understand why her own sister had passed herself off as Elaina and tried to have the princess, Trevan's daughter, killed.

"Think about it, all the tainted blood that runs in our world. Half fae, half mortal, half vampire, dark fae," she prattled on. "Who is even real anymore? They need to die before they come for us all."

She had gotten no more than that from her sister who had refused to speak further, and honestly, Elaina had been too distraught at the entire situation to press the issue. Now, with a clearer mind, she thought back to what she knew of Hetus and why the fact her sister had referred to half vampire and dark fae. The history she had learned was that Jarrah had created the vampires and Micah had evolved them and somewhere her own grandmother, Nina, had gotten involved. This meant that the vampires carried fae magic because fae created them. Was that what her sister had meant?

"Good morning, Elaina," Storm pulled her from her thoughts.

She focused on the new queen of Glenmoore, who wore a short green dress that matched her eyes and black leggings. Her auburn hair was in a single braid, and a simple gold band studded with emeralds sat atop her head. Since she had been here, Elaina had never seen Storm dress extravagantly as many royals often did. Storm was very much down to earth, and it was evident that the vampires loved her, and none would hesitate to lay their life on the line for the new fae queen.

"Morning, Majesty." She decided now was better than any other time to ask her questions. "May I speak freely?"

"Of course. You and I are family."

It was true. Storm was the daughter of Nina, Elaina's grandmother, and while they did not share the same paternal ancestors, Storm was her aunt. "I have a question about the vampires."

"Go ahead. I will answer if I can."

"There were never any females, were there?" She watched the queen's body language, which went slightly stiff but only enough for a trained observer such as herself to even notice.

"My understanding is that originally, no. The vampires Jarrah created were male. Of course, that means when Micah tampered with their DNA, he only had males to deal with. I assume mortal women became fated mates to the evolved vampires, so they bore offspring. But, as you know, that all happened before I was born."

"You assume, but there is no evidence that mortal females and not fae were the first to bear these children? Harper spoke of the fact that there are no females in Hetus except for the fae, and the mated females, which have all been mortal. Why are no females born?"

"I do not know why, and the only person who would know is long dead. Why do you inquire?"

"Forgive me, I'm only trying to understand why my sister committed treason. Something she said has me wondering how the vampires bore children in the earlier days if they had no females. Who is Lucien's mother?"

"Lucien's mother was mortal. A fated mate to his father."

It was possible that was what her sister meant when she referred to half vampire. Except, she understood that when a mortal mated with a vampire, she transformed. Her humanity lost. It was also possible her sister was deranged, and that was something Elaina was going to have to live with.

"Is it possible that some of the earlier vampires mated with fae?"

"I suppose in the early years it is possible, but there is no record of such. Would it matter?" Storm asked.

"No. Of course not. Thank you for your time, Majesty." She curtsied, then continued on her way with this nagging sensation deep in her gut. Why would it matter? She wasn't sure, but for some reason it did, and she intended to first find out exactly how the vampires were created, then follow the trail to wherever it led. She had to know if these creatures were trustworthy and the perfect place to start was back in the library at the palace in Drudora.

CHAPTER 2

Lucien still felt the cold sting of Elaina's words. They had only been here a few weeks, and she had no trouble letting it be known that she did not trust any of the vampires one bit. Did he blame her? She only knew the stories she was likely fed as a child. He had spoken to a few fae from Drudora who had come to Glenmoore to help, and they all seemed slightly edgy around him and his men until reassured they would not become a meal. He decided the best thing to do was to speak with Storm and see if she might offer some advice.

He slipped back inside and followed the scent Elaina had left behind. A trail of intoxicating jasmine that made his mouth water to taste her. The trail led him right to Storm, who was about to step into her private apartment.

"Majesty." He bowed his head. "If you have a moment, I would like to speak with you."

She smiled. "Lucien, I held you in my arms when you were a babe. I always have time for you. Come in." She opened the door, and he followed her into a modest living room. It spoke of Storm's taste, which had never been grand when she lived with them in the palace in

Hetus. It seemed nothing had changed now that she was queen of her own territory.

"Have a seat. Would you care for something?"

"No, thank you." He folded himself into a dark blue chair and leaned back, waiting while she sat across from him on the sofa.

"What can I help you with?"

Did he just blurt it out or warm up to the subject? "I have dreamed of my mate." That was a little warm up.

"That is wonderful news!" She clapped her hands together. "I know you were beginning to worry."

He shook his head. "No, it's not, because my mate is Elaina."

Storm blinked thick lashes over her green eyes. "I'm not even going to ask if you are certain because I know you are." She wrung her hands. "You should know she was asking questions."

He stiffened. "What questions?"

"She asked about the females and, in particular, who your mother was. Of course, I told her your mother was a human fated to your father." She leaned forward and her voice dropped to a whisper. "She referred to something her sister said that had her questioning the matter, but she never indicated what."

His heart pounded. "Do you suppose the sister found out?"

"I don't see how when the only ones who know are you, your brothers and myself. The rest are dead."

He shifted, now uncomfortable in his chair. "If it should ever get out who my parents really were…"

She paled. "Our people could not withstand the war that would ensue."

"You're certain there is no documentation?"

She shook her head. "Your mother is dead and buried in an unmarked grave, and everything I couldn't burn is with her. As for your father, there is no evidence to who he really was." She leaned back in her seat. "Your royal parents rest in their respective place below the palace and the library holds the falsehoods Micah weaved together. He was careful to cover his tracks, I will credit him for that."

The tomb Storm referred to held the couple who had been passed off as the king and queen and as his parents. Micah had hidden his actual mother like some kind of dirty laundry, and it was difficult to swallow. She had deserved so much better than the life that had been handed to her. He had grown up loving his parents, only to learn that his entire life had been a lie. A dark, dirty secret that threatened the very existence of himself and his two brothers, Andrei and Dorin. If it were simply the three of them that would be wiped out, they might consider coming forward, but thousands of lives were also at stake.

"This entire thing was the doing of three very selfish fae." Storm's anger filled the room. "I never understood my mother's greed and why she sought to send two brothers into a feud."

Lucien sympathized. Storm had grown up also thinking she knew who her parents were. Her mother, Nina, had solicited the love of two brothers, Jarrah and Micah. When Nina had chosen Micah, that was when the war began. The two fae lovers moved to the territory called Hetus, and that prompted Jarrah to create the vampire demons to annihilate his brother and the fae who had followed them. Micah, however, had used his own magic to evolve the DNA of the vampires and while everyone believed that Lucien and his brothers were born of these evolved beings, they were something entirely different. Oh they held all the same abilities as their brethren. Each had a wolf and bird spirit they could shift into. They survived on blood just like the others, but that was where their similarities ended. The brothers held a dark power that they kept buried deep inside them. So deep that not even Storm could detect it.

The day when Micah lay on his deathbed was when Storm learned her father was really Jarrah. It was also when Micah confessed what he had done but gave no reason why. Storm covered the tracks Micah hadn't and took the then teen boys under her wing. She told them the actual story and took them to see their birth mother. He recalled the beautiful female with the long black hair who looked upon her three boys with a mixture of love and sadness. Love for the children she bore and hatred for their father, a man Lucien despised just as much.

Storm taught them why they must never speak of their real parents or what they were. She was the one who guided them into adulthood after his adoptive parents passed on, and it was Storm who hid the truth from everyone. She had as much to lose as they did and lived with the demons that her own mother and uncle left for her.

"I wish I had the answers, but I don't. How can I claim a female who despises what she thinks I am and still expect to keep this secret? Andrei was lucky that fate chose a mortal for him, but a fae..." he shook his head. "How can I lie to her for our entire life together?"

"I assume she doesn't suspect that you two are fated?"

He laughed. "By the way she looks upon me, I'd say no."

"May I touch you?"

"Part of me wants to tell you no out of fear but go ahead." Storm held the fae power of vision and often saw things when she touched people. It was how she knew Harper had not only been Roman's mate, but that the mortal was half fae and the daughter of King Trevan. Storm's gift was spooky convenient.

She moved to stand beside him and placed her hand on his shoulder. It only took her a minute before she stepped back with a distressed look on her otherwise beautiful face.

"I see a lot of darkness ahead for you, but also light. I fear there will be many paths for you to choose from, but I can't tell you which to take."

"Great, that is not helpful."

"I am sorry, but you must trust fate knows what she is doing. At the same time, you need to watch Elaina, for I fear she will not let her questions lie dormant. Perhaps your pursuit of her will put her mind to something else?" She grinned.

"Yeah, most likely taking my head off." He got up and headed for the door. "I'll come up with a plan." Then he stepped into the corridor. What a mess. But there was only one thing to be done about it. It was time to confront his mate and establish exactly how she felt about him. He just hoped his hide didn't get singed.

ELAINA HAD SHOWERED THE SWEAT AND BLOOD OFF HER FROM training several fae and vampires to her style of fighting. She'd taken a little too much pleasure in causing pain to the vampires when she'd shared exactly what a fae of her status was capable of. They had stood their ground, and she was confident they would do well in protecting their new queen. They were loyal to Storm, and for that she was grateful. Loyalty was one thing Elaina understood. She had sworn her own allegiance to King Trevan when they were children growing up. It was probably the reason she had such a hard time with why her sister had betrayed them all. She needed to understand the reason behind it, or she would never rest.

A knock came at her door and forced her back to the present. She walked over and opened it only to find the vampire prince, Lucien, taking up space on the other side. She probably feared this vampire most of all. They considered him a prince. Named so by Micah long ago, and she was certain that the vampire royal family were special in some way. They had to differ from the rest of their kind. It was the way of royalty.

"What do you want?" Her tone held an edge of civility.

"We need to talk."

She crossed her arms and tried not to notice how well his black T-shirt stretched across his broad chest. No. She was not noticing that one bit. "Fine. Speak."

He arched a dark brow. "I am not having this discussion with you from the hall."

"And I'm not inviting you in and giving you the freedom to enter whenever you wish."

"What the hell are you talking about?" His brows dipped down, giving away his frustration, and it was clear his patience was wearing thin.

"The invitation. If I don't give it, you can't enter."

He laughed, moved her aside and strode past. "You seriously believe in mortal myths? Shame on you, I thought you smarter than that." He turned and leveled his sexy gaze at her. "I don't need a fucking invitation to go anywhere. Now, shut the damn door so we can have a discussion."

She contemplated tossing a magic blast his way but didn't want to trash her apartment, so she closed the door with a shove. Marching to where he stood, she stepped into his personal space and jabbed her finger at his chest, once again tying to ignore the hard muscles under his shirt.

"You have a lot of nerve storming in here like this."

"I knocked like a civilized man. It was you who took this to the next level by being a pain in the ass."

A red haze dropped over her vision, and it was all she could do not to blast him to hell and back. She allowed a sizzle of her power to leak out however and gave him a little tap.

He laughed. "That all you got?"

The haze she stared through darkened. "You do not want me to throw everything I have at you. Besides, it would upset Storm that I killed you."

"You can't kill me." This time he crossed his arms and widened his stance. Cocky fuck.

"That sounds like a dare." She would never admit that unless he threatened her or someone she cared about in some fashion, she wasn't a killer. Elaina might be a warrior and the king's guard, but she used violence only when necessary. She'd been known to capture spiders—which made her skin crawl—and release them out of harm's way. It was a soft side she allowed no one to see. It made her vulnerable.

"No dare, but I think we both know you won't do it."

She let out a snort. "If the air fills with any more of your ego, I might choke to death. Please, enlighten me."

"Because you can't kill your mate." The smirk on his face was both devastating and deserving of being slapped off.

"Have you been drinking?" Could vampires become inebriated? Fae got tipsy, but that was as far as it went.

"Fast metabolism," he replied, still holding his smirk, surrounded by a scruff of facial hair that had her wondering what it would feel like against her skin.

"Then you've taken a hit to the head. Perhaps you should go to the infirmary." She held down the panic that rose in her throat like a severe case of heartburn.

"I'm perfectly fine. It seems you're the one with an issue here." He gripped her arms because she still stood too close. "Yes, the man you despise most is your destiny." Then, before she could react, he crushed his mouth against hers. Pulled her so close that she wasn't sure where he began and she stopped. Gave her a sampling of the rough whiskers she had wondered about only seconds ago. Their bodies were one, and that's when the fire inside her lit.

She wanted to protest, to shove him away. Scream at him to get out of her apartment and never return. But something was wrong with her. She had no will of her own. It was busy playing naughty with the vampire who scraped his fangs across her lips.

No. No. No! This is all wrong!

Her mind might still be rational, but apparently it needed to have a conversation with her body, because it was having none of it. Thankfully, he released her and walked toward the door. Before he stepped out, he spoke.

"I'll leave you with that as well as this little tidbit. We claim what's ours, and you are mine." Then he was gone, leaving her shaken.

She touched her lips, her knees still knocking together. How had he done this to her? There was no way she was fated to belong to him. He disgusted her.

"Then tell your body that," she reminded herself.

Pacing, she searched her mind for some confirmation that he was wrong. Her body had never reacted so intensely to a male before, and she certainly wasn't without experience. Then she realized. Ever since Lucien and his brothers had come to the palace looking for their friend Roman, she had stopped sleeping with the king. She and King Trevan were fuck buddies. They had an uncomplicated relationship that under the covers they were friends and lovers. Outside, he was king and she his royal guard. It had worked perfectly for years. However, when Trevan had offered her a night of sex right before she left to come to Glenmoore, she had turned him down. Something that had surprised them both, and she had no explanation for it then, but now?

She collapsed into a chair and stared at nothing. "I cannot be a vampire's mate. I *will* not be a vampire's mate. There has to be a reasonable explanation for Lucien coming here and making such a claim." Then she realized how convenient his claim had been right after she had visited Storm and asked questions.

"He is hiding something, and I intend to find out what."

CHAPTER 3

The sweet smoky taste of passion. That was what still sat on his tongue after kissing Elaina. That fae was a frenzied storm mixed with soft curves, and both were a lethal combination in his world. He'd watched her fight, both physically and magically, and she stood her ground without issue, never backing down. The images of her in warrior mode made him hard. Would she be fire in bed? He had glimpsed her softness, however, and not just those luscious curves that had pressed against him. Inside her there was another passion. One that she thought made her weak, and that was the reason she kept it locked away. If she knew he had gleaned this information from just one kiss, she would likely try to cut his head off.

He would keep this little tidbit to himself for now, but he would use it to his advantage later if necessary. What he had to do right now was speak to his brothers and let them know Elaina was asking questions. He headed outside and into the sunshine. Several fae and vampires stood talking, but he only gave them a nod of acknowledgement as they bowed their head to him. He shifted to his falcon and flew toward Hetus, the weight on him was heavy as he understood the battle he was going to have claiming his mate. What the hell was fate thinking? While Elaina had softened against him when he kissed her, it had been brief, before she'd placed the icy shield around her that she always kept in place. It was going to take a chainsaw to chip through that cold exterior. Would she feel a mating pull toward him? Thoughts of her possibly with another man had his bird screeching into the cool air and wanting to hunt down something simply for the kill. He didn't give in to the urge. His bird only ever took prey when he was hungry, and right now he was simply pissed.

Thirty minutes later, he landed on the roof of the palace in Hetus. He shifted and used his senses to locate his brother Andrei, then headed down the spiral stairs to the second floor where he walked a much quieter hall to the private office his brother kept. When he reached the closed door, he knocked.

"Come in, Lucien," Andrei called.

Lucien twisted the knob and walked inside, happy to find his youngest brother, Dorin, sitting in a leather chair across from Andrei. The two appeared to be in conversation while drinking whiskey.

"I'll have one of those too, if you don't mind." He didn't even wait for a reply, but walked to the bar and grabbed the decanter, filling his crystal glass to half full.

"Bad day?" Andrei asked.

"You've no idea. It's why I'm here and glad to find you both in this room." He moved to a vacant brown leather chair and glanced to make sure the door had closed behind him when he'd entered. This private office was soundproof, so even if a vampire or fae stood outside the door, they would never hear the conversation going on inside. Thank fucking god, because these words were for their ears only.

"Storm informed me that Elaina was asking questions about our parentage." He took a gulp of his drink and relished the burn as it went down his throat. The pain helped him stay focused.

Andrei leaned forward, several creases lining his forehead. "Why?"

"No idea, other than she isn't a fan of vampires."

"What could she ever actually learn?" Dorin piped up.

"Storm was careful to hide everything, but there is always a chance something was missed." He scraped his fingers through his hair. "So, who the fuck knows." He met both his brothers' worried gazes. "And that's not all."

"What the fuck else?" Andrei asked.

"Elaina is my mate."

"Fuck us." Dorin got to his feet, emptied his glass, then went for a refill.

"Is she aware?" Andrei relaxed, if only slightly.

"I informed her just this morning. But, if you're asking has she had visions of us, I'm going with a firm no on that one." He took another gulp of his drink.

"This isn't good. She is not only a full-blooded fae, but a king's guard. I'm thinking that makes her more powerful than your average fae." Dorin didn't bother to take his seat again. His edginess made the room stuffy.

"You are correct about that. Her power is only lesser than her king. Storm has asked me to keep a close eye on Elaina and make sure she never discovers our truth."

Andrei grinned. "Well, considering she is your mate, tracking her should be a simple task for you."

"Ha. I'm not so sure, but I intend to do my best. However, I may need the two of you to keep me from killing Trevan."

"Everyone knows she's sleeping with him. I am sorry, but perhaps there is enough of a bond that she will forgo that activity in the future." Andrei was always the calm in their storm. Lucien had missed his elder brother terribly when Andrei had been cursed by a witch. No one in Hetus had known what happened or why their king and his royal guard never returned from the mortal realm. To make matters worse, the doorway to Romania had been closed to them. Both Lucien and Dorin had even stepped into Hungary and tried to shift and fly to Romania, but they quickly found themselves back where they started. They then attempted taking a plane only to have the same results. That country had a barricade around it that was impossible to break through, and it had been perplexing. After months turned into years, they assumed their brother dead. Lucien had taken Andrei's place as king and ruled. Every day had been torture for him, thinking his brother forever lost to them.

"We all need to hope, because if I catch them together, I *will* start the next fae war."

"First things first. We need to make sure she never finds out about our father and his misdeeds." Dorin brought them back to focus.

"I despise that man. It's been difficult to keep up a fake love for Micah and how he so grandly turned our ancestors from vampires to civilized men." Lucien laughed. "Considering he was anything but civilized himself."

Andrei nodded. "I often wish he had lived while I knew the truth so I could have killed him myself."

All three of them felt the same. While everyone knew the three princes' parents to be the king and queen of Hetus, the royal couple who had been installed by Micah and then the boys passed off as their heirs. Reality was a dark, dirty secret. While Micah had used a combination of his blood and magic to cause the vampire DNA to evolve into what the vampires were today, the three boys were different. Micah had kidnapped a dark fae princess from her world, kept her locked up and raped her repeatedly until she bore him three princes. The boys had been none the wiser until Storm had come to them when they were teens and revealed the truth. They were the royal sons of a dark and light fae. A forbidden union with even more forbidden offspring.

Two worlds that had been at odds for a long time. It was their understanding that their mother, the princess, was the last of her line. How her people hadn't known what happened to her was a question none could answer, but then not a lot was known about dark fae. However, if the dark fae ever learned the truth, war would ensue that would be so bloody the chance of survivors in this world would be minimal. There was also the possibility that the dark fae might want the three boys to come to their world and rule since they were now the only living link to their princess. Again, no one knew for certain.

If that wasn't enough of a train wreck, the truth in this world would have the light fae wanting to slaughter them out of sheer fear. Andrei, Lucien and Dorin held more power than most fae or vampire. They were the product of two powerful fae families and their magic combined. Not even the three of them were fully aware of what they could wield, because they kept that part of them under a magical lock.

"My biggest concern is how do I keep what I am from my mate?"

Unlike your mate, Andrei, who was human before you met, Elaina is a powerful fae. Will she sense the darkness inside me once we are joined?"

"I do not know," his brother replied, and it didn't make him feel any better.

"That is my fear. One side of me will claim her no matter what, and consequences be damned. The other... It lives in fear of it being me who causes the destruction of everyone we love and the life we hold dear." Hell, he wasn't even sure if the implosion of the fae worlds wouldn't spill over into the mortal realm as well.

Either way, he was fucked.

ELAINA HAD A LONG DAY TESTING THE GUARDS WHO WOULD BE THE first line of defense to the queen of Glenmoore. Once she was certain they were at their peak, they could then recruit the rest of the queen's army. It wouldn't be many, but Storm had the backing of Hetus and Drudora should it ever be needed. It was unlikely, however. With the opening of the borders, peace was upon all of them. Still, she couldn't ignore this nagging feeling in her gut as she crawled into bed. She was grateful for one small thing; she hadn't seen Lucien for the rest of the day. The prince had set her every nerve on edge and it was all she could do to not search for him around every corner she turned.

As she fell into sleep, her mind entered the dream world and that was the beginning of her nightmare.

Fires encompassed the landscape, and the air was heavy with acrid smoke that caused her to cough even though her mouth and nose were covered. Magic, thick and black, coated everything and she knew it could only be one thing.

Dark fae.

They had infiltrated their realm and destroyed nearly everything in their path. But why? Elaina ran as best as she could toward the palace. She needed to get to King Trevan and make sure he was safe. She should have never been out of the palace in the first place. Had she been at her post... She dared not even think about it.

As she entered the palace, the halls were deadly quiet. Servants lay in pools of blood, and Elaina had to navigate around them. There wasn't time to mourn the loss because panic pushed her. Was she already too late to save her king?

She raced for the throne room, instinct telling her that was where she needed to be. When she flung open the doors, the horror nearly sent her to her knees. Her king lay in a pool of blood, his head detached from his body, and sitting on the throne was...

She dropped to her knees, blood splashed around her and rippled away. The gaze that greeted her was intense and one she knew all too well. He was dressed in black from head to toe and wore Trevan's favorite crown. The sad thing was, he looked like he belonged on that throne.

"Why?" she whispered.

"I did not choose this destiny; it was forced upon me. I tried to tell you to leave things be, but you refused."

She brought this on? "I wished for none of this." She wept. "Who survives?"

"The queen of Glenmoore, but she has been stripped of her titles. We have taken the princess of Drudora prisoner. You can imagine the impact that has had on her mate." He stood, tall and full of anger as he took the steps to her. She looked up at him. He was raw power; hard lines etched his handsome face, and his gaze was filled with regret and pain. "Thousands of your people are dead."

He rolled his fingers into fists. "You will have to live your life knowing what transpired here. For that, I am sorry."

"I am the royal guard to the slain king. I should join him as your enemy."

His lips twisted until his fangs were exposed. "You will not die, mate. I tied your fate with mine when we bonded." Then he walked away, his boots splashing blood as he left the room.

Elaina jolted awake. She touched her chest and tried to slow her racing heart. Her breathing was far too fast, and she feared she might actually pass out. "What the hell was that?"

Her king lay dead, and Lucien sat on his throne. It was twisted and wrong. There had been a power inside him that was dark and deadly. How had the dark fae come to enter the equation? They had held peace with their deadlier counterparts for many years. They simply ignored each other and stayed away from the dark fae realm. As her breathing slowed, she examined every aspect of her dream. Lucien was supposedly her mate, or so he had tried to indicate earlier.

What did she believe the truth to be on the matter?

Elaina was a smart and reasonable woman. Fate had already proven that a vampire and half-fae could be destined. It was feasible to believe that a full-fae might be the mate to a vampire as well. How did she feel about Lucien? If she dropped her barriers and searched, she found a deep attraction to him. She had studied him from afar. The way he moved was like a beautiful wild animal. She had even witnessed him shifting into his wolf, and the beast was magnificent with its coat of sable and black. The wolf held the same intense dark brown gaze as Lucien, and there was no mistaking they were one and the same.

Lucien was only a few inches taller than her, but his build was that of a lethal fighter. He was muscular, yet nothing like the human body builders she had seen in the mortal realm. His dark blond hair seemed ever changing in color, just like the spirit animals he held inside him. His falcon was a sight to behold when he soared the skies above the palace.

"For the love of the goddess." Her heart was racing again just thinking about the vampire. Was he her mate? The possibility was very real. Just the way her body reacted to him was a good indicator that his words might hold truth. Not to mention the time when one of the fae from Storm's court had stood a little too close to Lucien and flirted with the vampire. Elaina had wanted to tear the female's head off. The entire event had set her on edge because it was simply ludicrous that she even noticed, let alone wanted to act upon it.

But why did he show up in a dream as a dark fae king with the blood of her own king at his feet? Perhaps she needed someone to help her decipher the meanings behind this. She looked at the clock. It was early morning, but sleep was no longer an option for her, so she rose from bed and headed for the shower. Her schedule was open today, so it was the perfect time to seek an old friend of hers who might shed some light on this situation.

CHAPTER 4

While Lucien wasn't able to jump into the mortal world like Elaina, he was adept at following her scent. Crossing the mist from his world and into the mortal plane, he quickly shifted into his falcon and took to the sky. His mate had come to New Orleans, a city filled with magical beings and a place he also found himself attracted to. Here, anything was possible, and mortals tended to either look the other way or they embraced the magic themselves. He traced her steps to the garden district and to a small cottage with a black iron fence surrounding the yard. The sun showed it was mid-morning, so he landed on the fence to the back of the yard and looked around.

A box garden holding herbs and flowers filled the small area, along with a few benches and a table. It was there that he spied his mate sitting with a redheaded female. He remained in a position where he couldn't be seen but could watch them. The female poured what appeared to be lemonade into tall glasses and the two drank and laughed. Something about the female was familiar, and that was when he realized it was Korinna, the witch who had assisted Andrei in breaking his curse. Oddly, he hadn't known that Elaina knew the witch, but they appeared to be old friends. He tried to tune into their conversation.

"The dream was simply terrifying. What do you suppose it meant?" Elaina asked.

"Hard to say. Could be your subconscious rebelling at the idea that this vampire is your mate. Do you have a gift of vision?"

"No. At least I never have before, but I can't help thinking he is hiding something."

Lucien picked up his head, not liking those words one bit. She had a dream? It seemed he had come too late to hear the details, but apparently, he had been part of it. He rather liked the idea that he was invading her sleep. Maybe it meant she was finally connected to him. He continued to listen.

"Is it possible a gift like that would show up now?" Korinna asked.

Elaina shrugged. "It's not common, but it has happened. Sometimes a gift will show itself at a time it's needed then vanish later."

"Then you should pursue answers. While I know Andrei and helped him break his curse, I don't know the family enough to tell you they don't have something to hide. Especially if you are not comfortable with the situation between you and Lucien."

Elaina snorted. "How am I supposed to be okay with what he is? I've lived my entire life believing the vampires are our enemy. Fate is asking me to flip a switch on my emotions."

Korinna gave a nod. "That's usually how it goes. It is understandable that you're having difficulty, but you will come around, I'm sure. Fate is never wrong in her choices, and believe me, I've seen many matings in my lifetime."

"I'm not ready for this. For him. Not until I know who he is, no matter what fate says."

Lucien understood Elaina's feelings. He was nothing like her. Where she was light and magic, he was dark and dangerous. An outcast in her society where only a few had been accepting of the vampires. It would take years to undo what two fae brothers had done and if his secret was discovered, it would only prove why the Vladimir brothers should be feared. Somehow, he had to show her he was to be trusted while keeping her from discovering who he really was. His only other choice was to walk away from the female he had waited so long for, and that was something he wasn't sure he could do. Every fiber of his being wanted her. Only death would cure his craving to have her as his own.

It was a cruel irony fate played.

The women were getting to their feet, and it looked like their little party was ending, so he took off to a nearby tree where he could watch Elaina. It was obvious she was going to seek answers, and he wondered if they could plant some in her path. It was an option that should be considered. The two women hugged and then Elaina vanished.

Damn it!

She'd jumped, and this time he did not know to where. He could assume back to Glenmoore, but until he got there himself, he couldn't be certain. Monitoring his mate was going to prove challenging and might call for some extreme actions on his part. As he took off from the tree, he swore he heard the witch below giggle. Did she know the falcon was him? His bird species was usually present in this area in the summer months so he was kind of a fluke for bird watchers. As he winged through the sky, the temptation to use the power that sat idle inside him was immense. He could make a jump and follow Elaina, but to do so would likely come with consequences. He might tip off other fae once he unleashed any of his magic, and that would lead to terrible things. For now, he would make his way back to Glenmoore and speak to Storm about how they could lay out some false facts for Elaina to discover and hope it was enough for her to end this madness.

ELAINA POPPED DIRECTLY INTO THE LIBRARY IN DRUDORA'S PALACE. The room was three stories of books, most of which were works from the world's well-known authors, but that wasn't what she was after. It was the tomes stored in the back room under a magical lock that she wanted to see. Jarrah's own account of his reign in Drudora and how he created the vampires. Elaina had never been curious enough to read the texts herself, learning what she needed to know from the teachings of her childhood. However, considering the current changes, she felt it was time to make sure nothing had been missed in those teachings.

Slipping up the stairs, she walked to the end of a row of books and touched a sensor on the wall. The wooden panel slid to the side, and she stepped into a small vestibule. Once the panel slid back into place, she placed her palm on another sensor that allowed her access to everything behind the thick glass door. With the door open, she walked into the room. The lights coming on ahead of her, she moved to a small wooden table and a single chair. The chamber was no bigger than most walk-in closets, and to the right of the table was a bookcase that held leather journals labeled by year. She scanned the tomes until she found the correct year and pulled the thick book from its shelf and placed it on the table. Taking a seat, she carefully opened to the day in their history that their king, Jarrah, had created the vampire and started reading.

"Princess Renna has paid back the favor owed to me with a vile of her blood."

"Princess Renna?" From what they understood, the princess was the last of the dark fae royalty. At least if their spies were to be believed. The princess and her family had perished, leaving distant family to rule the dark fae world. Elaina wondered how Renna owed King Jarrah any kind of favor. She went back to reading.

"Today, I combined my blood with Renna's using the following spell. *Uin dúr a uin galad. Thiw nin aiqa a thiw cín aiqa, nin gúl apvieno na tolth- i raug na ceri- nin imperium.*"

"Well, the spell seems simple enough. Nothing unusual about it." Basically, Jarrah had used his magic to combine the blood of the two fae, thus creating his vampires. The vampires were a creation of magic and blood, and the sketches on the next several pages revealed creatures with large, pointed ears and a long face. Their eyes were wide set but small and bright blue. There was no nose to speak of, more of an opening on their disgusting face. When she stared at the mouth, a wide gaping maw filled with pointy teeth and four enormous fangs, she shivered. It was difficult to imagine that Lucien had evolved from this.

So, how did Micah perform such a miracle? That was the million-dollar question. It would have taken a very powerful spell and probably more blood from Renna to reverse what Jarrah had done. Just the simple fact that the princess had given blood so freely had Elaina questioning this text. The only thing the two fae had in common was warring with each other. Otherwise, they had been enemies as far back as any fae could recall.

Elaina and her people were referred to as the light fae, and their creator was the goddess of light, Itasis. Light fae used nature and the earth for their power, and if they took too much, nature always healed herself. Her people also looked more like mortals, with their varying hair and eye colors and skin tones. The only actual differences were the pointed ears, their height tended to be taller than the average mortal and fae were exceptionally beautiful.

Dark fae, on the other hand—from what little she had learned—were created by a demon. Their skin was fair, hair always black, and all had blue eyes. They were a beautiful people, as she had seen one once when she was a little girl. A male had been captured in their realm and publicly executed. Dark fae wielded some dark powers and rather than take from the earth, they worshipped the moon. They also drank blood, which explained the vampires. If Jarrah used light and dark blood to create his vampires, it would stand to reason the creatures would carry traits from both fae. She wondered, though, where the spirit animals that the vampire held had come from. To her knowledge, neither fae had such powers as to transform into an animal. Glamour? Yes, they all had the ability to look different, but that was nowhere near the same.

She closed the book and placed it back in its spot. The only thing she had gained from this was more questions. How was she going to go about finding the answers she sought? Was it likely that Storm would have them right in her own library? Well, she would simply have to look. If there was nothing to hide, then the tomes would be there as fae were excellent record keepers. Heading out of the small chamber, she made her way back through the library and into the main hall. She thought briefly of seeking Trevan, but then decided against it. The idea of turning him down for a good fuck wasn't something she wanted to do again. Just the thought of sleeping with the king put her on edge, which made her even more edgy. She never said no to sex and now that Lucien had staked his claim, it left her wondering if there was something to it. Another thought that left her nerves frazzled. It was a feeling she despised. Elaina was in control at all times.

Except now.

She made the jump back to Glenmoore where she landed in her room. Taking a moment to compose herself, she found it difficult since the scent of that damn vampire still hung in the air. It did something to her, and if she were honest, it heated her entire body. She flopped onto the couch.

"Why would fate choose a vampire as my mate?"

Lucien had to be playing some kind of game with her. She didn't like games, but she was an expert at them. If Trevan caught wind of the possibility that she was the mate to a vampire prince, he would insist she pursue it. The king would take her denouncing her own mate as a slap in the face to him and the crown. The only way out for her was to prove Lucien unfit and being a vampire would not cut it. Not now that there was peace among them. She got to her feet, more determined than ever to find dirt on the vampire who held way too much sex appeal.

Flinging open her door, she checked the corridor, almost fearful he would be lurking nearby. There was no one around, so she headed to the library. The palace of Glenmoore held almost as many books as did Drudora. She supposed Micah and Storm had recorded just as much history. Once inside, she quickly scanned the books until she found a section titled Hetus's history. There were half a dozen thick books on the shelf. She picked up the first and flipped through it. Disappointment flowed through her when she discovered it was nothing more than a record of births and deaths. No mention of vampires so she shelved it and grabbed the next. As she scanned the pages, she spotted the name Andrei and her heart beat a little faster. It listed his birth date and his parents, who were the king and queen of Hetus. Under that was an entry for Lucien, then another for Dorin, the youngest brother. The last one on the page were the deaths of both the king and queen. There was no indication as to what the cause was, however.

She flipped a few more pages, but it was more of the same, so she put the book back. Taking the next, she discovered it to differ from the first two. This was a recording of events, so she searched for the time when Jarrah had sent the vampires to Hetus's door. When she found the first entry of the vampires, she grew excited. Taking the book, she went to a nearby table and sat down. Page after page she read of the gory blood bath that had ensued, and part of her was angry that so many fae had died at the hand of her king's father. Sure, they had followed Micah, but it had been her grandmother who had put a wedge between two brothers. Elaina held no love for Nina, unlike her now dead sister who apparently had worshipped the woman. She wondered how Storm felt about her mother, Nina, when she discovered the lies about who her real father was. Nina had spread herself between the two brothers and passed Storm off as Micah's daughter when in reality she was the child of Jarrah. It might explain why Micah had chosen vampires to become the royals of Hetus over his own daughter. It would be a nice slap in his brother's face. When the truth had come out, it appeared Micah had known all along but loved Storm as his own. Just not enough to crown her queen of his territory.

She gasped when she finally reached the entry she had been looking for. Reading word for word, she chewed her lip as if waiting for the plot to a storyline to be revealed. According to the entry, Micah had used his blood and a spell to remove the dark fae blood from the vampires, which propelled their DNA into a fast-forward evolution. However, it seemed he could not remove all the dark fae from their genes, which might be why they still needed to drink blood. As another experiment, he chose three vampires. Using another spell, he bound those vampire's souls to the kings of Hetus then fed them his own blood, which seemed to cause a faster transformation. Roman had been one of those vampires, which explained his loyalty to his king. The other two names were Cristian and Taos.

Leaning back, she took a breath. It made sense, the text in the book. Micah had been a powerful fae, same as his brother Jarrah. She wondered though why there was no mention of the first king. Why was Lucien's father chosen for such a role? There had to be something special about him, otherwise Micah, being a prince, would have ruled himself. This bothered her, since it was highly unlikely any royal fae owning his own territory would transfer kingship to another. Especially since he had a daughter—even if she wasn't his blood—and the transfer of power wasn't to another fae.

Something was up with this, and it required further examination.

CHAPTER 5

"She is in our library as we speak." Lucien paced the floor, unable to sit still while his mate was busy trying to dig up his past demons.

"She will only find what has been written for all eyes to see," Storm replied.

"Elaina will not stop there. I overheard her speaking of a dream that terrified her, but I was too late for the details. The witch asked her if she had a gift for vision. You and Elaina share a maternal line, is it possible she also shares your gift?"

Storm seemed to contemplate before replying. "Nina had the gift and passed it to me. I didn't know my elder half-sister, Elaina's mother, as she was already mated and lived in Drudora when I was born. It's possible she also had the gift and would have passed it on to Elaina. Considering Elaina's station with the king, I would surmise that both her parents were powerful fae. Her father was a king's guard, and those titles are normally passed down to their children because of the magical bloodline."

Lucien growled, and Storm tilted her head in question.

"The mention of Elaina's station. She is fucking the king, you know?" The act of saying it out loud caused his body to tense and the darkness that lived inside his soul to beg for release. Killing something right now was all he could think about. That and locking his mate in a room where she could not escape. The only thing keeping him in check was the fact that he had located her in Drudora, but fortunately, she had only been in the palace library and never went to see her king.

Storm's brow arched high. "You know fae are highly sexual beings. I am not surprised that she would be the king's concubine, considering her position."

He growled again. "You're not helping."

She sighed. "Were you expecting a virgin?"

"Of course not. I simply don't wish my mate to be fucking other men!"

"I'm sure her body has recognized you as hers, even if her head has not."

He recalled how she had softened against him when he'd kissed her. "Perhaps I need to use that to my advantage."

The queen laughed. "Be careful. Fae are skilled in the art of seduction. It is why mortals often summon us." She rose from her seat and walked to where he stood. "When was the last time you fed? You look pale."

"I'm not even certain. Not since I first saw Elaina."

"You cannot allow yourself to grow weak. The tenth full moon is in three days' time and you need to be at your prime in order to perform the ritual."

"You're right, of course." Every ten full moons, he and his two brothers had to summon power from the moon to help keep their identity hidden. They, along with Storm, went to a remote area in the mountains and performed the ritual.

"I'm tired of hiding. All this sneaking around, performing rituals is going to come to a head one day."

"Until the time that the two fae can get along, you and those after you will need to use caution."

"What will become of my children? Andrei's offspring will probably present as vampire, but mine? Considering my mate is a full-blooded fae, and I am what I am, our offspring might be difficult to explain."

There was every possibility his children would present dark fae genes. How would it look if they were born with the fair skin, black hair and blue eyes known to dark fae?

"I wish I had all the answers for you, but alas I do not."

"What about the dark times you saw in my future?" He was feeling like one edgy vampire, and that was never good. He despised being out of control and at the moment he was on a roller coaster from hell.

Storm was close enough that this time she touched him without asking, not that he minded, unless of course, she was going to present him with more shit news. She closed her eyes and was quiet for several minutes before she finally stepped away and spoke.

"I see nothing that concerns me. Perhaps I need to use this gift on Elaina and see if she presents anything different."

He wasn't happy with her reply. "What do you see, exactly?"

"Nothing different from before."

"Yet it doesn't concern you?"

"I know you will make the right choice when the time comes."

Well, he was glad she had so much confidence in him because he sure as hell didn't. While he wasn't happy, there was nothing to be done about it. "I will go see what my mate is up to. I sense her still in the library and will bet she has located the history of Hetus."

Storm smiled. "That is to our benefit then."

He gave a bow, then excused himself. As he was walking to his destination, he crossed paths with Cristian who had volunteered to come in place of Roman who was busy setting up house with his new mate, Harper. While he was in a hurry, he stopped to chat.

Cristian tipped his head. "Highness."

"Cristian, have you spoken with Roman?"

"Yes. His new mate has kept him busy painting their new home." The vampire rarely cracked a smile, but Lucien swore one broke free. Slightly.

He laughed. "I have a hard time seeing our friend covered in paint rather than blood."

"I can attest that it presents an odd image since I witnessed it myself. He seems happy though."

Lucien smiled. He craved that same happiness and cursed the fae who refused to simply be obedient. Truth be told, though, he preferred her exactly as she was. Full of fire. "I shall have to pay them a visit and see this for myself."

"Be prepared. He is not the Roman we once knew." Cristian tipped his head again. "Good day, Highness."

"Good day." Lucien continued on his quest and a short time later entered the library where Elaina was shelving a book.

"Did you find what you came looking for?"

She faced him and threw on a smile. "Your family tree is interesting."

"How so?"

"Well." She sauntered closer and rested her hip on the edge of the table. "I didn't see any mention of your parents, I mean how they became the king and queen that is. Why would a fae of royal blood choose another to rule in his place?"

He decided this was a perfect time to get into her space. He stepped closer. "You didn't read far enough. My father, Evan, was a highly respected vampire who Micah chose to lead us. My mother, Sadie, was his human mate. Andrei was born a year after they mated. I came two years later and Dorin another two years after me." He raised a brow. "Satisfied?"

"I suppose." She gave a light shrug of her shoulder as if she was indifferent to the entire situation.

He knew better, however. Having enough of her little games, he moved even closer, leaned down and planted his palms on either side of her, caging her in. He brought his mouth within inches of hers.

"If you're looking for a way out of this mating, it's not happening."

"You think to force me into this?" Her eyes widened, but the emotions that filled the room were anything but shock. Why did she think she could play him for a fool?

"I won't need to. You cannot deny what's between us." Without hesitation, he claimed her mouth. She sent a small jolt at him, but it was so slight he shrugged it off. Instead, he responded by pressing into her until she was leaning back on her elbows and his erection was at her core. The heat they gave off had him fearful the sprinkler system might send a shower of water down upon them. While he wouldn't mind seeing his mate soaking wet, he wasn't about to ruin the books in this room.

She parted her lips, and he took advantage. Staking an even deeper claim. The taste of fire sat on his tongue, but it wasn't as one would expect. There was no bitterness. His mate was more like red hot candy. Sweet, spicy, intoxicating. He swore she stifled a moan, and he deepened the kiss.

She never tried to push him away, and he had to fight off a grin. It wasn't until he scented someone approaching that he released her. Stepping back, he allowed her to compose herself.

"The next time, I will have you coming so hard you will beg me for mercy." Then he walked away, leaving her to whatever thoughts bounced around in that beautiful head of hers.

ELAINA LET OUT A LONG BREATH AS SHE WATCHED LUCIEN WALK away. Admittedly, his ass was as fine as they came encased in a pair of jeans and it heated her entire body to the point of critical. She stood, straightened herself and ignored the look cast at her from the fae who had entered and was pretending to browse the books on the far wall. Elaina had found nothing useful in her search. The last entry was where Micah had appointed a vampire named Evan as the king, just as Lucien had said. From there, it was a matter of him mating with a human called Sadie, and the rest was history. Perhaps there was nothing to find and her sister had been delusional.

She walked to the door and left the vast shelves of books behind her. Her mind was a complete mess after that kiss, and it made her wonder why she had allowed it in the first place.

You enjoyed it!

She would freely admit to herself she had and also wondered what he was like in bed. If there wasn't any dirt to dig up on him, then was there a reason not to sample the goods? It didn't mean she had to commit. Her willpower was much stronger than the vampire gave her credit for. A grin spread over her mouth as she made her way back to her room. One thing Elaina loved was a good sparring match. Both she and Lucien were warriors to the core, and she had watched him practicing with the others. He was good. Very good, but what she had in mind was more of a mental battle. One of wits which seemed fair since she was technically more powerful than him in the magic department. She never wanted to be accused of taking advantage and knew Lucien to be of equal mental intellect.

Behind her closed door, her smile widened. "So, you think you hold all the cards, vampire?" She laughed. "We shall see who breaks first. I know there has to be something behind your parents."

She headed for the shower and was quick to clean up, then dry her hair so it fell to her shoulders in soft blonde curls. Next, she donned a red negligee that fell to the floor. The slits up either side allowed her long, lean legs to show. The best showcase was her breasts. They were covered in red silk and lace that threatened to expose her pink nipples. Checking herself in the mirror, she slipped on a pair of silver, open-toe heels to complete her look of seduction. In the living room, she picked up her cell phone and shot off a text to Lucien. Seduction was one thing fae excelled at and some might call this an unfair advantage given to Lucien. However, was it her fault the male would take the bait?

Lighting candles, she also made sure the fireplace was burning warmly before grabbing two crystal glasses and the bottle of red wine she'd been saving for a rainy day. When she placed them on the coffee table, a knock sounded at her door.

"Perfect timing." She sauntered over and opened enough that he could not see all of her.

"Your text said you needed to see me?"

"Yes. Come in." She stepped behind the door, allowing him in, then closed it behind her. When he turned to face her, he did not show that her state of dress surprised him. However, the lust that rolled off him gave him away. So did the rising bulge in his jeans.

She walked past him and went to sit on one end of the sofa, making sure there was plenty of room for him to sit next to her. "Wine?" She held up the bottle.

"Why not?" He sat next to her. "So, what game are we playing now?"

She laughed and filled both glasses. "No game. You intrigue me and you must know that fae have a..." She handed him his glass, allowing her fingers to brush his. "Healthy sexual appetite." She pulled back and studied his face. Lucien was a handsome man, there was no doubt about that. His eyes reminded her of mocha with only a hint of milk that darkened to black when he was pissed or, in this case, aroused.

"Are you saying you wish to fuck?" His brow cocked upward as he leaned back into the cushion, about as relaxed as a wolf ready to attack its next meal.

"You left me in quite a state earlier. I thought it fair to offer you the chance to rectify that before I went elsewhere."

His gaze turned ice cold and his nostrils flared. "How thoughtful of you."

She shrugged, then sipped her wine, realizing she was playing with fire. "Well, you are the one who keeps insisting that I'm your mate." She crossed one leg over the other, allowing the silk to fall away and expose long, lean muscles. God, she loved the art of seduction. It heated her blood. Heightened every sense she had. "Unless of course, you think I might be too much for you."

He leaned in closer and grinned. "What makes you think I've never fucked your kind before? I'm a prince and well sought after in my world."

Prick! She contained her emotions, knowing full well he was testing her. She hated the thought of him with another female. Still, his nearness was enough to melt her panties had she been wearing any. "I can be demanding and hard to please."

His smile widened as he set his glass on the table. He then reached for hers. "Don't want you to spill this." Then he set it down, pushed her back into the cushions and slid his palm up her exposed leg.

Heat seared her skin. "This does not mean we are mating," she whispered.

He bent his head and kissed between her breasts, then lifted to stare at her. "No mating. No making love. This is fucking. Raw, hard, and fast, fucking." Something sinister swirled in his eyes. "I will show you no mercy. So, are you certain you wish to play this game with me?"

She swallowed the moan in her throat. Had she gotten in over her head? Too late now, her body was wound tight, and she needed release so badly it mattered not that he was a vampire. Matter of fact, the knowledge of it made her even hotter.

CHAPTER 6

For the first time, he felt her emotions, which were a jumbled mess of arousal, fear—and when he'd mentioned other women—anger. He focused on the arousal and began kissing the column of her long neck. His fangs ached to sink into her, but he thought better of it. Biting her was something he was going to have to ease her into. His mate still held an apprehension for vampires. He did, however, allow his fangs to scrape her delicate skin, soliciting a moan from her.

It only caused his cock to throb harder.

He leaned back, gripping the silky fabric holding her breasts from his view. This female would only understand one thing from him right now. He tore the red silk until she lay bare all the way to her pelvic bone.

"Hey, I liked this gown."

His only response was a growl before he latched onto her pink nipple. His tongue flicked until it hardened in his mouth. She dug her fingers into his skull.

"Yes," she hissed.

The room filled with her lustful perfume, and the heat that rolled off her threatened to burn him. Seemed his mate liked things hot, hard and dirty. Well, he could live with that and tossed out his previous reservation on biting her. He pierced her nipple with the tip of his fang while he slid his other hand to her sex. She was hot and wet, and he wasted no time in slipping two fingers inside.

She bucked.

Her muscles contracted around him as she nearly turned him to ash. Moving to her other nipple, he gave it the same attention which caused her to grind hard against his hand. He circled his thumb over her clit, and she dug into his scalp even harder, pulling his hair. He plunged a third finger inside, showing her no mercy. Fucking her with his hand as if it were his cock. She cried out, and he knew she was on the verge of coming. He pulled back and watched the heavy rise and fall of her chest while she stared daggers at him.

"Don't worry, I'm not done with you yet." He gripped her ankles and pushed her legs wide then dived in. The taste of her on his tongue was enough to drive him to his knees had he not already been there. He licked through her folds before flicking over her clit and slipping his fingers back inside her. He was desperate to make her orgasm on his tongue. To hear her cry of pleasure and only seconds later he fulfilled his desire when she cried out. Her muscles flexed around him as her orgasm took hold of her. Not giving her a moment to catch her breath, he pierced her clit with his fang and sent her over the edge again.

"Mercy," she cried out. "I'm begging for it."

He released her and smiled, licking her pleasure off his lips, then his fingers. "You are delicious, but your mercy is only temporary." As he stood to undress, a knock came at the door.

Her eyes widened. "I should see who that is. It might be important." Before he could growl out a reply, she was on her feet. Gone into her bedroom and back with a robe on, securing the tie as she went to the door.

Great, why did he feel like he was going to have to take care of this raging hard-on himself?

Elaina could hardly walk, her body wrung out from the intense orgasm, but somehow, she got to the door and cracked it open. Outside was a messenger from Drudora. He handed her a piece of paper, then was gone. She closed the door and opened the note.

Meet me at the tower at midnight. I was a friend of your sister, and I have information that might interest you.

She folded the note and shoved it into her pocket. She had only an hour before the meeting.

"Everything okay?" Lucien asked from the sofa.

She focused on him. The vampire was a seduction overdose and damn it, she still wanted to fuck him. Was dying to become intimate with the erection between his legs, but there wasn't enough time. She was going to have to take a raincheck because this meeting was important. She had to be prepared for anything once back in Drudora. For all she knew, it was a trap.

"I must go home and tend to an important matter. I am sorry." She moved closer. "Can we pick up where we left off later?"

He stood and crushed her to his hard chest before she could even gasp. His mouth once again laid claim to hers. This man was everything demanding and raw and she would swear he held no softness at all except she had witnessed him with the children. He was gentle, giving them sweets and telling stories. It was as if he had a twin who was the total opposite of him.

His kiss ended abruptly as he pressed his hard thickness into her. "I fully expect that and more when you return." Then he walked to the door and left.

Heading for her bedroom, she braided her hair then stepped into the shower for a quick rinse. Dressed in leather pants and a black tee. She strapped a dagger to her thigh and a short sword to her back, then donned her leather jacket. With still thirty minutes before her meeting, she jumped to a location near the required destination and flared out her senses. There was nothing out of the ordinary. Most fae were asleep, but some still worked in the palace. Rather than jump to the tower, she decided on the long way and walked since it would allow her the ability to detect any traps. She had no idea what her sister had gotten tangled up in, but she had paid for it with her life. Elaina needed to find out more for the sake of her sister than anything else.

She finally made it to the tower when she sensed another fae in the shadows. "Come out so I may see you," she commanded. If this fae knew even the slightest about her, they would know she was lethal.

A tall figure stepped closer until she recognized his face in the moonlight. "Elaina. Thank you for meeting me."

"Marcel, why did you not call a meeting with the king on this matter?" Marcel was king Trevan's spymaster, and anything he or his people learned was reported directly to the king. It was odd that he would meet with her.

"I don't wish to bring this to his attention until I know for certain."

"Then start explaining." She remained alert for any intruders, but it was unlikely. She trusted Marcel. Had known him for many years. Yet, she had to wonder how he had gotten tangled up with her sister.

"Your sister came to me about six months ago with the information about the vampires and how she had a way to control them." He held up his hand to stop her from speaking. "I know. It sounds bad, but she convinced me that the knowledge she held would aid us. I did not know she planned treason against the king."

Elaina crossed her arms. "Let me guess, you were fucking her."

He cast his gaze downward before he met hers again. "Yes."

She rolled her eyes. "The women in my family seem to have a gift for using sex to get what they want." Hadn't she just done the same with Lucien? Yeah, she kinda had. "Continue."

"Cassia believed the royal brothers are the sons of Micah and…" He looked around, hesitant to finish. "The dark fae princess."

"What?" She stepped closer. "Do you mean the two had actual sex, and she bore him children? It sounds ludicrous."

"I mean exactly that."

"Do you have proof of this?" Her heart pounded. If this were true, then the brothers had to be destroyed. The small part of her that knew Lucian was her fated mate fractured.

"Unfortunately, I don't have documented proof, but your sister had a contact in the dark fae world who reported that their world had been plunged into civil war many years ago. A family member killed the king and sold the princess off to a light fae. Apparently, the people were hopeful their princess was still alive."

She had to blink to be certain that this wasn't a dream. The conversation was too wild to be believed. "So, it's thought that Micah was the one who bought her?"

"It is, and your sister suspected that the three royal vampire brothers were in fact Micah and Renna's sons."

Well, well. Now that was information that was interesting indeed, but proof had to be found. Still trying to wrap her head around what she was hearing, she asked, "But what would be his purpose in that?" She met Marcel's gaze. "To destroy us?"

"Most likely. What other reason would he have?"

"Do you know the status of the dark fae currently?"

"My spies tell me they eventually killed the king, but now his son holds the throne. I don't think things are well for the dark fae."

"Do you think if they knew the princess had three sons, they would seek them out? If for nothing than to reclaim their throne?"

He shrugged. "The brothers are direct descendants of the dark fae princess, but they also carry the blood of our kind. I suppose it would depend on how desperate they were to bring back the old royal blood. Accepting a half-light fae king would be a pretty big ask for their people."

She moved to the window and looked out at the moonlit night. If everything Marcel said was true, then why had she not sensed fae within Lucien? He would be a full-blooded fae and should wield the power as such. He was hiding it, or this was a tall tale and she had to find out the answer. She faced the spymaster again.

"Yet the brothers present as vampire, though I guess we hold no knowledge what an actual coupling between fae species would produce. I can tell you that Jarrah used his and Renna's blood to create his demonic version of the vampire. Micah then used his blood and some reversal spell to rid them of the dark fae DNA. It worked to a point, and that is where you have the vampires of today. Except for the three he bound to the kings of Hetus by having them drink his blood."

She tapped her finger to her lips. "Now, the tomes I read in Glenmoore led me to believe the brothers were all born to a vampire named Evan and his mate Sadie. The king and queen of Hetus."

"Why would a fae prince name a vampire king of his territory?" Marcel asked.

"Why indeed?" She sighed. "And bigger why, why have three sons with your mortal enemy?"

"Two enormous questions that need an answer."

She moved closer. "If I am to follow him, then I need a concealment spell."

Marcel smiled and pulled something from his pocket. It was a simple amber stone encased in gold on a piece of leather. He handed it to her.

"Wear this and use the spell, *im lill i fuin na gollo nin in cerc*. You will fade into the darkness unseen."

"I will the darkness to cloak me in its embrace? How fitting." She slipped it over her head and tucked it under her shirt, the warmth of it settling between her breasts. "Do you suppose it's possible the sons have no idea who they really are?"

"It's possible, but we have no way to know what seed Micah may have planted deep in their minds. They are a ticking time bomb that must be stopped. Even if they do not know, at some point the dark fae will discover them and we will be the ones to pay the price. They will not care that we were not directly involved in the wrongdoing of their princess."

She stared out the window again. "You are right, of course." The images of her slain king and Lucien sitting on his throne came flooding back to her. She now understood the meaning behind it and the words he had spoken to her.

"I did not choose this destiny; it was forced upon me. I tried to tell you to leave things be, but you refused."

Did that mean her actions would be what started a war? Her fate was tied with his. She recalled him telling her that as well. If her dream were to be believed, then what she did today may cause the fall of her people in the future. She would have to take care and make her choice once she had more information. For now, she would head back to Glenmoore and figure out the rest from there.

"Thank you for bringing this to my attention. If you find out anything more, please contact me."

"Certainly." Marcel vanished, and she made the jump back to her room at Glenmoore palace.

CHAPTER 7

Lucien hadn't seen Elaina since the messenger came to her door with a piece of paper that had caused him to leave with a raging hard-on. He wondered if the news was that dire or if she was simply avoiding him. Did she regret what had transpired between them the other night? His mood grew pissier by the moment, and there was nothing worse than a vampire pissy because of his mate. Been there and seen that movie with his brother Andrei and his friend Roman. Why did females insist on bringing out the dark side of their fated males?

He needed to pull his shit together because in a few hours he and his brothers, along with Storm, would have to perform the ceremony that hid who the Vladimir men really were for another ten full moons. He was tired of hiding who he was. Keeping a knot around his powers was becoming bothersome, yet he understood what might transpire if he chose not to. He didn't want others to perish because of his actions. He'd lived with his cursed life for nearly seven hundred years. What was an eternity? Still, he was torn. He wanted Elaina, yet he feared hiding the truth from her. She already looked upon him with distrust and if she knew his true identity...

It was something he shoved to the back of his mind. He and Elaina had made progress the other night. He would curse his soul for eternity if it meant he could be with her.

"Vampire."

Her sweet voice stopped him in his tracks and snapped him out of his funk when he turned and met her deep blue eyes.

"Elaina." He tried to judge her mood.

"I am sorry about the other night. I'm afraid I got tied up in business, but all is good now." She moved closer, placing a palm on his chest which seared him to his very soul and did nothing for the boner in his pants. "I hope we can still pick up where we left off." She smiled.

He tried to keep his heartbeat steady. "I was thinking you were avoiding me."

"Never," she purred as she walked her fingers up and down his chest. "Free tonight?"

Damn. Tonight, they had to perform the ritual. "I have some business that will take me away from Glenmoore, but I will return tomorrow and then I'm free."

She gave a nod. "Tomorrow night then?"

"My place or yours?"

"I'd love to see how you live. Your place."

"As you wish. Until tomorrow."

She then did the most unexpected thing by raising her chin and kissing him. It wasn't a long, deep kiss, but it was still full of her passion and was enough to make him stand taller as she walked away from him. Tomorrow night might as well be a century away, but he would think of her tonight tucked in her bed while he was out worshipping the full moon.

Pulling himself back to the task at hand, he had two hours before he had to meet up with the others to begin tonight's ceremony. Heading to his apartment, he took a quick shower then dressed in dark jeans, a black shirt and boots. He looked at the garnet on his right ring finger. Each brother had a ring of sliver with a large square blood-red garnet. Claws that represented their spirit bird held the stone in place, and on each side was the head of a howling wolf. Storm had the rings made right after Micah had died and the terrible truth had come out. His mother then spelled each stone, giving them protection and a way to help hide their fae magic. He would never forget that moment in time.

She had touched his cheek after placing the ring on his finger and offered a tired smile.

"My son. I see inside you to the man you are. You are nothing like your father, as your heart is pure." She leaned closer. *"You will one day avenge me, for you are a true dark prince. You carry more of me than your brothers, which gives you the right to take back my father's throne."*

Those were the last words she ever spoke to him, for the next day he had found her with a knife in her heart and a note next to her stiff body. She had taken her own life.

Storm had buried Renna in an unmarked grave, and Lucien never shared what his mother had told him. Guilt, mingled with anger, rode him daily because he should avenge his mother, yet he also needed to protect those he loved. He was at constant odds with himself as to what to do. He knew he should confide in his brothers or Storm, but the words never seemed to come out.

Looking at the clock, he should head out if he was going to make it on time. He opened his door and stepped into the corridor. The place was quiet yet he sensed someone. Looking around, he saw nothing, so he walked toward the nearest exit from the palace. Once outside, the strange feeling disappeared, so he shifted to his falcon. Soon he was airborne and flying toward Hetus, where he would meet up with his brothers so they could journey to the mountains of their home together. The moon was bright, its golden-white glow lighting up the world.

Once in Hetus, a raven and a snowy owl took flight beside him and the three headed to the same location, deep in the mountains. Storm had found them a place in a large crevice where they wouldn't have to worry about being spotted. The ceremony required a bonfire, and magic would be thick in the air for several minutes.

Lucien landed and shifted, as did his brothers. Storm was already there and had a six-foot fire started and was walking around it, chanting and tossing sprigs of herbs into the blaze. He stripped his shirt and tossed it to the ground. It was now or never.

It had been tricky following Lucien, but Elaina had managed by doing the one thing she hadn't wanted. She used the connection they had started the other night to help her locate him. Her wrist itched, reminding her of the price she had paid. Thin gray lines swirled in a delicate pattern with a very faint outline of a bird in the middle. She had learned from Princess Harper that the mates of vampires bore a mark, and even though she and Lucien hadn't had actual sex, their foreplay had been enough to start the process. At first, she had freaked-the-fuck out before coming to realize she might use this in her favor. Reaching deep, she had found the thread that led to Lucien and followed it.

The lines on her wrist darkened.

Whatever. She had to find out what was going on and if what the spymaster had told her held any truth. The story was plausible. The dark fae had been in turmoil for many years from what she had learned, and it had taken only a small coup to seize power, sell the princess and kill the king. She could almost feel sorry for Princess Renna. Many thought Micah to be the crueler of the two brothers, and she could well imagine how the princess had spent the rest of her days.

Settled into the shadows cast from the fire, she stood silent and observed. Lucien pulled his shirt over his head and bared the most heavenly set of abs she had ever laid eyes on. She nearly snarled at herself as she moved in for a closer look. It wasn't as if she'd never seen him without a shirt before. She had plenty of times and had always tried to ignore the fact. Now, with the mark on her wrist throbbing, it was difficult. He was all masculine godliness in dark jeans that sat low, revealing well-defined muscles that led straight to the place she had wanted to explore most.

She shook her head, angry that she would allow him to distract her in such a way. She was a warrior, and to remind herself of that fact, she slipped into combat mode. Her king and those he served were counting on her to keep them safe and failing at that mission was unacceptable. She would take Lucien's head if necessary.

Are you so sure about that?

She told her inner voice to zip it and pressed on.

The three brothers, now naked, stood at three points around the fire, and Elaina tried to harden herself against the thick member between Lucien's legs.

Seriously? Being naked has to be a requirement for this little party? She encased her desires in a block of ice and focused on their actions, reminding herself she despised the vampire. To help, she pulled a dagger from each thigh and held them in her palms. The feel of her favorite blades brought comfort as well as helped ground her. These daggers had been the cause of much bloodshed over the years and had served her well.

When she caught Lucien playing with something on his finger, she moved closer. She had seen the ring before but had never paid it much attention. It was made of silver with a square garnet held in place by what appeared to be claws. Bird claws, perhaps? She glanced at the brothers and noticed they had matching rings on their right hand as well. Being so close to Lucien, she also took a better look at the falcon tattoo in attack mode on his right bicep. It was exquisite and caused her to lean in closer to study the detail. That was when he whipped his head to look straight at her. She gasped and held perfectly still. Staring into his eyes, she was so close she watched them swirl from light brown to black with flecks of gold. His nostrils flared, and he took in a deep breath while she held hers. She dared not even blink. Did he see her? Marcel had assured her that the necklace would keep her safe from prying eyes.

Elaina, you idiot! He couldn't see her, but she was his destined, and it was probable he felt her presence. Might even catch her scent if his breathing was any indicator, and that was when she noticed that glorious cock between his legs thickening. She took a slow step back, then another and a few more until he finally moved his gaze back to the fire. Damn, that had been a stupid move, but she was in unfamiliar territory when it came to mates and even vampires. Or, in this case, a potential fae who lived in the world of both light and dark.

The brothers looked up at the moon, extended their arms as if reaching for the glowing orb, and began speaking.

"*I galad -o i ithil na- nin rod plural rodyn. I fuin -o dú nin polod. Thiw i ceocfo -o anntu im gwedhi- niierte im am tovon in nin faer a awaui o ignpin esee.*"

Their words transfixed Elaina. *The light of the moon is my power. The darkness of night my strength. With the forces of nature, I bind everything I am deep in my soul and away from prying eyes.* She repeated in her mind, but the words meant nothing to her. She wondered if this was specific to dark fae and would have to see if she could find anything like it in the library. Maybe Korinna could offer some insight. Before she could go down that rabbit hole, the men dropped to their knees and drew symbols into the snow as they continued the chant.

The fire roared like a wild animal angered by someone or something entering its territory. Sparks exploded into the air and rained back down right before a demonic entity with blood-red eyes lifted from the center of the fire. Smoke billowed in the wind that had whipped into a frenzy. The black-skinned creature pointed a claw-tipped finger at Lucien and spoke in a language she didn't understand, but its voice came out in a thunderous clap and Lucien folder over, his face contorted in pain.

Elaina stiffened, her nails digging into her palms, and when Lucien roared in pain, it was all she could do to keep her feet planted where they were. Something deep inside her had her wanting to rush forward to aid him, but soon enough he lay in a panting heap on the ground and the creature focused its attention on Dorin. Soon all three men were left a trembling mass, and the demon was gone. The fire died down to its original size and Storm went to Lucien first and helped him to his feet, handing him a bottle of water. While he stood on shaking legs, Storm administered the same assistance to the others. A few minutes later and the men were dressing while Storm threw snow on the fire to snuff it out. The only light now came from the moon that hung brilliantly in the sky. With no words between them, Storm vanished, and the men shifted into their birds and took to the sky, leaving her alone to inspect the site closer.

CHAPTER 8

Lucien woke stiff and sore, as was the norm after the ritual. Calling upon the dark demon required a sacrifice where they gave up a small piece of their soul. How many more times could he and his brothers do this before they lost themselves completely?

He rolled out of bed and shook the fog from his brain. He could have sworn that he not only felt Elaina, but her scent had surrounded him. Of course, it had to be the fact that she was his fated because she had been nowhere to be seen. Not to mention that her being there was ridiculous and nothing more than his deep desire for her to be his.

He opened the glass door and turned on the shower. Stepping under the hot spray, he finally eased the tension in his sore muscles. Tonight, he and Elaina had a date to finish what they started a few evenings ago. He had to admit; she was full of surprises. Maybe this mate thing wouldn't be as difficult as he'd originally thought. Still, he had to make certain she never tried to dig into his reality any deeper. Stepping out, he dried, then looked at himself in the mirror. The mark left on his chest last night was nothing more than a raised pink line now, and by tonight when he and Elaina were together, it would be no more. The darkness inside him was buried for another ten full moons. As he stared at himself, he wondered what it would feel like to allow his true self to rise to the surface. What powers did he and his brothers hold? He was positive he could jump like the rest of the fae and probably summon power to zap someone, but what special gift did he hold? Fae seemed to have special abilities unique to individuals. Storm could often see visions when she touched someone. He recalled one fae who lived in Hetus who could tell an object's history by touching it. Storm had once told him that not all fae had special gifts. It was a roll of the dice when a child was born what, if any, they would end up with. Royal blood was always more powerful too. Of course, they didn't really know the dark fae that well and what powers they held other than summoning demons.

Walking out of the bathroom, he tugged on jeans and a shirt, wondering what the true intent was behind Micah's siring him and his brothers. It was something they had never figured out, and not for lack of trying. All three of them, along with Storm, had searched for a reason to no avail so they simply assumed it was out of spite for his brother Jarrah.

A soft knock came at his door and he wondered who the fae was he sensed on the other side. It was still early, and many wouldn't even be stirring yet. He moved and opened the door to find a fae, dressed in black, her face hidden in the darkness of a hood. His senses told him she was different, yet he couldn't place how.

The fae bowed. "Prince Lucien, I have a delivery for you." She held out a small package wrapped in plain brown paper.

"Who sent you?"

"Your mother." The fae tossed the package at him, then vanished before Lucien could utter another word.

Stunned, he watched the package fall to the floor and land at his feet. He quickly swiped it up and searched the corridor with both his sight and senses, but there was no one. That fae was gone. He shut the door and on the other side he leaned against it, his nerves slightly jarred. The package wasn't much bigger than a watch box and covered with plain brown paper.

"My mother?" He wondered what kind of trick someone dared play on him and was hesitant to open it. Still, it intrigued him, and he pulled the paper away to reveal a black box with an embossment on it. The emblem was of a gold half-moon and soaring above it was a bird. The symbolism was lost on him, as he did not know what it meant. Pulling off the top, he stared at a soft black cloth that he pulled out and unfolded. Inside lay a blood-red crystal cut and polished to a brilliant shine. Clasped around the top of the stone was a silver-etched crown. Small wings extended up on either side and were encrusted with red stones, and in the center was a falcon head with diamond eyes.

"What the hell?"

It wasn't a crown he had seen before, but he had a bad feeling about it. Moving to the kitchen table, he sat and laid the stone down. Shaking the cloth, he hoped something else might fall out, like a note. He looked inside the box only to find it empty.

"Fuck." Then he had an idea. Using his fingernail, he ran it along the inside bottom and caught a loose edge. Lifting, he peeled the layer back to reveal a piece of paper. He pulled the note out and opened the single fold. The handwriting was elegant and definitely had a feminine touch.

Lucien,

There are some things you need to know. Back home, I had a life. I had a mate and a daughter. My father, your grandfather ruled as king and life was peaceful until one day my brother took that away from us. He slayed my mate and my father. I was able to send your sister, Amber, into hiding before my brother sold me to the highest bidder who was your father. I do not know why Micah wanted me to bear his sons, but I am now glad he did.

I am certain my world is still in peril, and I'm begging you to make things right. I sensed the darkness inside you was stronger than the others. It was stronger than my own, and like myself, you hold the falcon as your spirit bird therefore you are the rightful heir to my throne.

I know this choice will be difficult for you, but my people will embrace you and your brothers. You are the dark fae king, use the stone to claim the throne and honor my memory. Save our people from the imprisonment they face. Save your sister.

Your loving mother,
Renna.

His hands shook as he stared at the note. Of course, there was every possibility this was fake, yet the paper smelled like her. Brought back painful memories of the short time he had spent with her. He was torn. Did he go to Andrei and Dorin with this? Storm? Or just ignore it? Was the fae who had dropped this on his doorstep his sister? What fate had befallen her?

"Fucking hell!" He scraped his fingers through his hair, his gaze landing on the pendant. It drew him to it, and he found himself unable to stop from reaching over to pick it back up. He lifted the leather cord over his head and tucked the stone under his shirt. The feel of the crystal against his skin was warm, much like his mother's touch had been. His decision was made. The first thing he would do was to seek a fae named Luna. The female was adept at reading objects. He just hoped this didn't cause him more trouble. Lucky for him, however, she lived here in Glenmoore after having followed Storm from Hetus.

He pulled on his boots, shoved the note along with the box in a safe place, then headed out the door. The palace was bustling with activity, so he slipped out a side door. He decided since Luna lived a couple of miles outside of town, he would go for a run. Shifting, he allowed his wolf to take over. Everything changed once he was on four paws. His senses became sharper, and every detail of his surroundings registered in his mind. Taking off at a run across the palace grounds, he enjoyed the soft lush grass on the pads of his paws. Rain scented the air showing a storm was brewing to the south and would likely reach them later in the day. He welcomed the rain. It always cleansed away the staleness and left everything fresh again.

When he spotted Luna's cottage in the distance, he stopped and shifted. Though he knew the fae well, he didn't want his wolf to startle her. Walking closer, he spotted her in the garden tending her vegetables. She rose and looked his direction, no doubt sensing his arrival.

She gave a curtsy. "Prince Lucien." Her blue eyes were wide with curiosity. "To what do I owe such a pleasure?"

"Luna." He tipped his head. "I have a piece I would ask you to look at for me."

"Of course." She smiled. "I would be happy to. Come in and I'll fix us some tea." She tossed down her gardening gloves and led him inside. Her cottage was small but neat and clean. He often wondered why she chose to live so far removed from the others. She was a beautiful fae, her dark blue eyes striking against her strawberry blonde hair.

"Please, have a seat." She indicated to the chairs in front of a cold fireplace. He chose the one closest to the door and sat down, removing the pendant from around his neck. Luna appeared with a silver tray and placed it on the table between the chairs. Pouring, she handed him a cup, remembering that he took his tea plain. Lucien had never been much for anything sweet.

"Thank you. You didn't have to go to all this trouble."

"It's no trouble at all." She sat and eyed his hand. "Is that the piece?"

"Yes." He offered it to her, and she accepted. Luna turned the crystal over in her hand before she wrapped her fingers around it and closed her eyes. It was only a few seconds before she spoke, but it felt like forever to him.

"This stone belonged to a dark fae. Royalty." Her brows scrunched together. "I sense it is ancient. Perhaps a few thousand years and it has been passed down from parent to child. It holds significant meaning to the family members." She opened her eyes and handed him back the crystal. "Lucien, this is something powerful and an item I believe the dark fae would want back in their possession." Her shoulders relaxed once he had the piece back in hand. Her gaze met his. "The one who bears that stone will hold the throne. It is not something you want to keep."

He tipped his head in acknowledgement. "Did you see who last owned this piece?"

She picked up her cup of tea and sipped. "A dark fae. Beautiful woman, I see the name Renna attached to her, but another female has held it since her. A daughter perhaps, and for some strange reason I saw amber." She shrugged. "I'm not sure why an amber stone would have any meaning."

Somehow, he kept his features from giving away the emotions that ripped him apart. "Thank you. I will be sure to heed your advice, as I certainly don't want the dark fae to have reason to war with us." Now he had to figure out what to do next. His choice would affect many lives.

CHAPTER 9

Elaina could not think clearly all day. Yet, she trained with the fae who would become Storm's royal guard. The queen had chosen wisely, as Blaise was not only as lethal as Elaina, he was loyal to his queen. Soon she could go back to her own king and her duties in Drudora. As she walked to her apartment, she reviewed her memories from last night. She was torn in half trying to figure out what to do. With no idea what the brothers had been doing last night, she wondered if it was some ritual to hide their identity. She sensed no fae blood in Lucien, but with what she had heard and seen, that meant nothing. The fact that Storm was involved had her torn as well. Storm was a fae. A queen now and sister to Trevan. However, Storm had spent her entire life living with the vampires and had watched the brothers grow up. Who was she loyal to? Elaina hated to think that Storm would betray them, but she had to keep that in the forefront of her mind.

Entering her apartment, she headed for the shower. Tonight, she would go to Lucien's place. Another thing she was torn on. Her body was still in a riot from their time together a few nights ago. Her mind couldn't stop playing the scene of him last night. He was hiding something. Would he come clean with her? As she stripped, leaving a trail of clothes behind her, she stared at the darkening mark on her wrist. The suddenness of its appearance had surprised her, and there was no one she could ask about it. To do so would align her with a possible traitor. Yet hadn't she already committed treason? She should go to her king with all the information she had to date. Instead, she was heading into the enemy's lair for a fuck.

Use this to gain information. Was she simply feeding herself a lie to make her feel better? As she stepped into the shower, she weighed the facts.

Marcel, the king's spymaster, had tasked her with information he wanted Elaina to try to either confirm or dispute. The information she had found in the Glenmoore library had left her with even more questions.

She adjusted the shower spray to a hard pulse, then turned her back to it. Planting her palms on the tile, the water beat between her shoulders and relieved some of the day's tension. Her mind once again wandered to her list: Marcel had possible inside information that the brothers were the offspring of Micah and Renna. Elaina had found nothing to either prove or disprove this. She had followed Lucien and watched as he and his brothers performed a ritual calling on the moon's power and some demon. It was a known fact that dark fae drew from the moon. So, last night was a step in believing that Marcel's information was correct. This left her with big gaping holes and from where she stood, there was only one thing to do. Gain Lucien's trust. After all, she was his fated and eventually he would tell her what she wanted to know. Would he answer her now if she came right out and asked? She still had to keep in mind the nightmare where her own king lay dead and Lucien's words to her that she had forced the issue. What did it mean? Instinct yelled that whatever move she made would be crucial to all. She would need to learn the truth and from there decide what path to take.

None of the choices laid out before her were appealing, but one thing was certain. Her job was to protect her king. If finding the truth and revealing it would be harmful to Trevan, then she would die with her secret. However, if saving her king meant killing Lucien, then that was a choice she wouldn't hesitate to carry out.

Elaina finished her shower, then dried off. She wrapped a towel around her dripping hair and went to her closet, pulling open the doors. As she scanned the items hanging, she decided to wear something simple, so she pulled out a summer dress. It was a wraparound that showcased both her breasts and small waist. Not to mention it was easy to take off. The yellow fabric fell below the knee but had a raised hem in the front. It was one of her favorites for its comfort. She paired it with soft leather slippers because heels might make her taller than Lucien, and tonight she was all about the demure female role. Placing the dress on the bed, she went to the box on her dresser that held her jewels and searched for the perfect bracelet to cover the marking on her wrist because she was certain the vampire would spot it immediately.

Time to apply her makeup, which again she went light on using only a bronzer and a lip tint that brought out her own natural color. She pulled the towel from her hair and fingered it until it was a mess of waves that made her look like she had spent the day on the beach. She stood naked in front of the mirror and slipped on the dress, tying it at the waist. All it would take was for him to grab one end of the tie and she would be fully exposed. On closer inspection, she noticed her nipples showed their dusky color through the light fabric since she had chosen not to wear a bra. That was when she forewent panties as well, leaving little to the imagination. She'd probably better jump to his front door, so she didn't cause too many heads to look her way. Not that she worried about such things. She was fae. They were sexual beings.

Putting the gold band on her wrist, she gave herself one last look and decided that she had transformed herself from hardened warrior to the perfect demure female. Only those that knew her would be wise to what lurked beneath her made-up surface. Not that she didn't like this role too. It was nice to become more feminine, but she seldom had a reason to do so. Smoothing her dress, she jumped from her apartment ready for whatever tonight brought.

THE VAMPIRE PRINCE

When the knock came at his door, Lucien set the filled wine glasses on the table and went to greet Elaina. Her scent already filtered through to him, so there was no need to question who was on the other side. It surprised him when he opened it and was greeted by a woman who had softened her hard edges. He had expected her to come in some slinky outfit with five-inch heels and looking like she was ready to kick his ass. Instead, she was all softness and now he couldn't decide which he liked better. He would have to sample them both to be certain.

"Come in." He stepped aside to give her room to pass by him, and that was when he noticed she wore no panties. Grinning, he decided he liked the naughty woman who thought to hide herself under a frilly dress. He could hardly wait to get it off of her.

"I poured us some wine. Please, help yourself." He followed her to the sofa where she took a seat and picked up a glass.

"A sparkling white." She sipped. "Mmm, sweet too, my favorite."

"I pay attention." He sat next to her. "You look lovely tonight."

She smiled. "Thank you. You don't look half bad yourself."

He laughed as he had on nothing more than a pair of dark jeans and a black button-up shirt with the sleeves rolled up to his elbows. It was then her gaze landed on the pendant that hung around his neck.

"That is unusual."

He shrugged. "Just an old piece I came across many years ago. It spoke to me, so I bought it." The lie that rolled off his tongue was like a dagger in his gut. He'd just told an untruth to his mate, and it nearly made him sick. What was he going to do when they were mated? Hiding anything from the one you were bonded to would be impossible. How did Andrei do it? It was then he wondered if his brother, the king, hadn't confided in Sonia. He was going to pursue this conversation later with his eldest brother.

"I like it. It seems to suit you." She took a rather large sip of wine before setting her glass down. "I've been hesitant to see you again."

"You still think I'm a villain?"

"I don't know what to think of you. I will admit, I am both attracted and fearful."

He frowned. "Fearful? You must know I would never harm you."

"I only know what I was taught growing up. You, or your people rather, slaughtered mine. You are the enemy who sought to annihilate Drudora."

Her words cut him. While she wasn't wrong, it was all in the past. "I understand. Perhaps that is why you and I have been chosen? First Roman and Harper, now us? It is time to heal both our people."

She nodded in agreement. "Yes, but what my sister did to Roman makes me question if it could happen again."

"I understand, but I cannot be controlled. I am my own man."

Her brow arched, and her eyes filled with questions. Likely ones he couldn't answer. "How are you different, exactly?"

He reached for her hand, laced his fingers between hers. "I am a royal, which makes me more powerful than the others. I made a vow to protect those who cannot protect themselves." Yet, he was still questioning overthrowing a dark fae king who did not belong on the throne. One who was responsible—directly or not—for his mother's fate and that of his half-sister.

"I understand you were king for several years. Your brother was away because of a witch's curse?"

"This is true."

She smiled. "I heard you were an excellent king."

"I had very large boots to fill. Andrei is our true ruler and each day I had to take his place was torture for me. Not that I found the task difficult, it was knowing how I had come to the role in the first place."

"You thought of the brother you had lost."

"Every waking moment." He took her hand. "I am sorry about your sister."

"Thank you. It was a hard task I had to carry out."

"Then perhaps it is time we put our pasts behind us." He leaned closer, raising her arm until he had it pinned behind her head, then he claimed her mouth. She offered no resistance but softened into him. It was when he moved his grip to her wrist that he encountered the gold bracelet and the power that pulsed beneath it.

His power.

He would bet his soul that if he tore the golden band from her wrist, he would find his mark on her flesh. She thought to hide it from him? Did she not realize that if they continued on the path they were on tonight, her marking would only darken? Each time they were together they would become more bonded. He should stop because he was traveling down a road that led to a dead end. She would find out his secret, and then what? Perhaps once bonded to him, she would keep his dark past to herself. But there was his mother and the pendant around his neck. He was bound to Renna as well and the bone-crushing urge to fulfill her request. Becoming king of the dark fae was out of the question, though. Doing so would reveal their true identity and place so many in danger.

Breaking the kiss, he stared at Elaina's swollen lips. He had waited so long for this female and she was here, right now, all soft, warm and willing. It was time to put everything else out of his mind and live in this moment. The path that lie before him was her and he would think of the rest later.

CHAPTER 10

Elaina wondered what was going through the vampire's head as he seemed to be deep in thought. Before she could think more on it, he stood, offered his hand and spoke.

"Let me show you the pleasures that await you."

The desire that burned in his dark eyes took her aback. Never had a male looked at her in such a way. Oh sure, men desired her, but what she saw in Lucien was much more than that and she had to admit it was a little frightening. He looked at her with the desire of a mate, and the mark hidden under her gold band matched the burn between her thighs. She slid her hand into his and allowed him to help her stand. Thinking he was going to lead her to the bedroom, it surprised her when instead he tugged on the tie that held her dress together and allowed it to open wide, exposing her naked breasts. Elaina was never one to question if she was good enough. That was a mortal emotion, but in this moment the man standing over her, raking his gaze across her flesh and burning her with his intense stare let her know she was more than enough. In his eyes she was everything, and it left bumps running across her skin.

When he curled his mouth into a smile and exposed his fangs, she suddenly craved them embedded in her flesh. Wanted more than anything for him to take everything she had to offer. He reached for her and pushed the dress off her shoulders until it pooled on the floor around at her feet. Just the graze of his fingertips on her skin caused her to let out a soft gasp. He stepped into her, gripped her chin and forced her gaze to meet his, and it was as if she had never seen him before. While fae were a beautiful people, this vampire was chiseled perfection, and she sensed a darkness deep inside him that both frightened and intrigued her. Did he hold the soul of a dark fae?

"*Cin obno na nin. Treneri- nin.*"

You belong to me, tell me. The words spoken in her native tongue caused a flood of heat to her core. He circled her nipple, and it hardened under his calloused fingertips.

"*Treneri- nin,*" he demanded in a low, quiet voice that was more of a growl.

She shivered. Elaina had never been one to be at such a loss. Giving control was not in her nature, but then again, she had never been with a male that made her want to hand over her most vulnerable self. She swallowed and spoke.

"*Im obno na cin.*" *I belong to you.*

He gave a satisfied grin, then lifted her off her feet. Cradling her next to him, the fabric of his clothes was rough against her skin and she wished him naked. Craved to feel every inch of him pressed to her and inside her. When he reached his bedroom, he laid her on Egyptian cotton sheets that caressed her in softness. He slid his hands along her thighs, sending heated electricity through her skin as he made his way down her calves where he carefully removed her slippers and set them aside.

Taking a step back, he unbuttoned his shirt, his gaze never leaving hers, and she rolled to her side for a better view. When he pulled the fabric free and tossed it into a nearby chair, she licked her lips. She had seen Lucien's naked chest many times in her days at Glenmoore. Had seen it up close last night when he was under the full moon, but nothing compared to this moment when he undressed for her.

The tattoo on his bicep flexed as he unbuttoned his jeans. Her anticipation filled the room while she watched him lower the denim to reveal his thick erection. Once he had stepped from his jeans, he moved across the bed and covered her body with his, being careful to keep his weight from crushing her. He kissed her. His tongue sweeping in and claiming every inch of her mouth. Fangs scraped her lips, then he gave a gentle bite. His mouth was hot against her skin when he kissed her neck and suckled lightly. She wanted to tell him to bite her, yet the words were replaced with a moan when he took her nipple in his mouth. His tongue flicked across it until it was so hard it was near painful. She dug her fingers into his hair, then deeper into his scalp as she moved her hips, trying to get the ache in her sex to subside.

It was no use. The only thing that was going to cure the pounding in her clit was for him to be inside her. Never in her entire life had she been this aroused. This out of control. Was this what it was like to want your mate? It scared the ever-loving hell out of her. She should be able to contain herself, but control had flown out the window and taken off to god knew where.

He kissed across her stomach, scraping those damn fangs the entire time until she expected scratches would mar her skin. It only made the desire for his bite that much more intense.

"You are cruel," she whispered.

He chuckled, and then his mouth was on her. His tongue soft and wet against her folds and when he flicked across her clit, she arched into him, her fingers gripping folds of sheet.

"Yesss."

He worked her until she was on the verge of pleasured pain and all she wanted was release. She would either come crashing down with the most intense orgasm ever or she was going to die. She didn't want to die. At least not without a smile on her face and that was when he sank a fang into her clit causing her world to explode into a kaleidoscope of brilliant colors. She swore a woman screamed somewhere in the distance, then realized it was her as he kept her in the beautiful world of pleasure. When he finally gave her mercy and allowed her to slide downward, it was only a brief reprieve. With no warning, he was filling her. Stretching her until she thought there was no way she could take more of him. Yet, she did, and he touched every nerve at her center.

Gripping her ankles, he lifted her legs wider and then he fucked her. He took everything she had and more until she was once again spiraling. Still, he wasn't done. As he thrust faster and harder, he bit her neck. His fangs sank deep, and each thrust matched every pull of blood from her body, and with it, it pushed her over the edge. She had thought he had given her an orgasm before, but she had been dead wrong. That had been child's play compared to the euphoria she experienced. Dear god, she really was going to die and the only reason she cared was because she would never again experience this much pleasure.

WITH THE SWEET TASTE OF THE BLOOD OF HIS MATE ON HIS TONGUE, he lost control. His release took over and sent a growl ripping from the back of his throat as he filled her with his seed. Several minutes ticked by before he could retract his fangs and seal the puncture to her skin. Slowly, he brought her thighs back to the bed and looked into her eyes.

"That was... Holy shit," she said.

He laughed. "I believe holy shit to be an excellent description." He pulled free, still hard and still ready to fuck her again. She was going to become a craving he could never satisfy. Rolling to his back, he held his arm out so she could tuck in next to him, then curled it around her shoulder.

"Did we not take care of your needs?" She ran her fingers across his abdomen.

"Most definitely, but this is what you do to me. I fear I will have a permanent erection when around you."

She lifted her head to study him. "I see. Well, in that case..." She untangled herself, slung her leg over him until she straddled him. Gripping his now throbbing cock, she poised the tip at her entrance, then slid down until she had taken him fully.

He gripped her hips and fought the urge to lift her, then slam her back down. This was her show, and she was in charge. Planting her palms on his chest, she lifted herself until he was barely inside her. He gritted his teeth and dug his fingertips into her flesh.

"Tease."

She offered a wicked grin but held innocence in her eyes. "I would never."

"I don't believe you." He groaned when she slid down his shaft so slowly it was the worst torture he had ever endured and proof that she did indeed mean it.

Bending, she kissed his chest and worked her hips. Unable to stand another minute, he held her in place and thrust in and out of her. Her climax was near, he sensed it so held his own back. He wanted her to explode, but then she did the unexpected. She bit him.

There wasn't time to stop her because it happened so fast and the second her teeth sank into him, his balls pulled tight. His release slammed into him and they both yelled out their pleasure. When they were spent, she sat up and looked first in his eyes, then at the mark that was already healing on his chest, then back at him.

"What have I done?" She scampered off him and pulled away a blanket to wrap around herself.

While vampires normally had to drink their mate near death before feeding her their blood to perform the actual bond, he wasn't sure in this case. He and Elaina had now exchanged blood, though she got little from her small bite.

"It was only a drop," she yelled. "Tell me I didn't just bond us."

Her words of panic sliced through him like a knife. "Normally, no. It takes more than what we have done to completely bond us." He moved from the bed toward her.

She backed away until she hit the wall behind her.

He grabbed her wrist and ripped the gold band from her flesh, turning her arm so he could see the inside of her wrist. There it was, his mark. "You were trying to hide this." He had to get a grip on his anger. It would not help the situation.

She swallowed, then looked down. "It's darker than it was before, and it burns."

They both watched as the lines thickened and darkened further. Circles formed in interlocking layers, and in the middle was the falcon. Clear as fucking day.

"Why didn't you tell me not to bite you!"

"Why didn't you tell me you desired to do so? Besides, this isn't normally how we mate." He ran his fingers over the black lines, and that was when everything locked into place. The panic that caused his heart to race didn't belong to him. It was Elaina's. He felt her every emotion, her every thought, including that one where she felt like a traitor. His gaze narrowed on her as she tried to send a power surge through him, and it fizzled out before ever reaching his skin. They stared at each other with wide eyes.

"What are you hiding from me?" she accused.

"I might ask you the same question. Why do you feel like a traitor?"

"Why do I sense fae in you?"

It was his turn to panic. Did she know what he was? "I say we dress, then we talk." He released her and walked away to grab his clothes.

"Excellent idea. I also need a drink." She scurried from the room since her dress was still on his living room floor.

By the time he dragged on his jeans and threw back on his shirt, buttoning it as he walked into the other room, she was dressed and pouring wine. Things had a little time to sink in, and he knew without a doubt they were bonded. Apparently, there had been no need to nearly kill her to do so. Was it because they were both fae? He was clueless on how fae mated. It had never been something he felt the need to pay attention to, even though he lived among many during his life.

He swiped up his glass and sat in a chair opposite her. Being close didn't seem like a good idea at the moment. After taking a swig, he decided he needed something stronger than wine. Getting up, he went to the liquor cabinet and pulled out a bottle of whiskey and two tumblers, then headed back to his seat. Setting the glasses on the coffee table, he held the bottle up and raised his brow at Elaina.

"Yes, please." She nodded.

He poured into both glasses, handed her one, then took his own where he raised it. "To whatever's next."

"I'm not sure I want to drink to that." She blanched but sucked back a rather big gulp. When finished, she spoke again. "I had no idea. I thought you had to drink all my blood until I was dead."

"Almost dead," he corrected.

She rolled her eyes. "Whatever. Dead, almost dead. Neither of those happened."

"I'm as perplexed as you. I honestly don't have an answer."

Her gaze narrowed until he swore she was going to blast daggers at him. "But I think you do know."

Fuck. Yeah, he probably did.

CHAPTER 11

At this point Elaina was ready to spill everything she knew in the hopes he would tell her his secret. She looked at the mark on her wrist that had finally stopped burning. Taking a deep breath, she licked her lips and thought about what to say.

"What do you mean you think I know?" His tone was demanding.

"I know what you are." Nothing like blurting it right out. No sense in fucking around. She was now mated to a dark fae and god only knew what kind of hellish nightmare this was going to bring down on all of their heads.

"Care to explain?"

Really? He was going to insist on playing this game? "Fine. I saw your little party last night. While I have no idea what you were doing, I have it on good authority that Micah bought Renna, the dark fae princess, from some family member who had started a coup by killing the king. The two of them sired you and your brothers."

He worked his jaw, and his pupils filled his eyes until they were solid black. His anger coiled in the room ready to strike and it sent a shiver of fear down her spine. If he was indeed dark fae, he could kill her with little thought.

"You say Micah *bought* Renna? Not that he kidnapped her? And get that thought out of your head right the fuck now. I cannot kill my mate," he growled.

"Yes. Her family sold her out. It is my understanding that while that brother is no longer alive, a family member still sits on the throne." She waited for what seemed like an eternity before he finally spoke.

"I was a teen when Micah died, and it was on his deathbed that he revealed who my real parents were. There was no reason given as to why he sired us." He laughed. "His ego, I suppose. It must have been quite the boost to have a dark fae princess in his possession. Though, we were under the impression that he kidnapped her. But either way, he locked my mother up and raped her until she bore him three sons."

His anger left a bitter taste at the back of her throat, and Elaina blanched. While the dark fae were no friends of hers, the princess didn't deserve the torture handed her. "I am sorry about your mother. Did you ever meet her?"

"Yes. Once we knew of her, we went to where he had her locked up. She was a beautiful, broken woman." He stared into the now empty glass he held between his palms. "We would have freed her, but she refused to leave, saying they had sealed her fate and it would only endanger us." The glass shattered in his grip as his lip curled into a snarl. "She took her own life soon after. Unable to stand the emptiness Micah and her own brother had left inside her."

"I am so sorry. No one deserves that kind of life." Her heart hurt for him and she had no idea what to do. This certainly wasn't the story she expected to unfold and knew there was more but waited for him to finish.

"Storm was the one who helped us hide the truth. We continued to let everyone believe the king and queen on the throne were our parents. She learned a spell from my mother before mother died that would help hide what we are."

"That is what you were doing last night?"

"Yes. We must perform the ritual on the tenth full moon. It keeps what we are locked away deep inside us."

"So, you are fae," she whispered.

"I am the combination of light and dark. Fear and hatred and a being that must hide in the shadows for fear of what my existence will bring upon others."

"Did you think if we mated, I would never figure it out?"

"I actually had hoped to keep it hidden. But things have changed."

"How? Because I mistakenly mated us?"

He reached under his shirt and pulled out the pendant he had been wearing. "This came via messenger with a note from my mother. She calls to me beyond the grave to avenge her and take my place as king of the dark fae."

"Oh fuck," she blurted out as the visions of her nightmare played in her head. "I had an awful dream recently. One that might actually be a vision. Though I've never had them before, the gift does run in my family."

"What was this vision?"

"I saw Trevan in a pool of his own blood, his head severed, and you sat on his throne."

He cocked his head. "Why would I kill your king? I have no desire to do so unless you're still fucking him."

She rolled her eyes but ignored his last comment. "It was what you said to me." Her hands shook, and she hadn't even realized that he had gotten up and moved to sit next to her. He cupped her chin and forced her gaze to his.

"What did I say to you?" His voice was quiet and soothing.

"You told me you tried to tell me to leave things alone, but I refused. Thousands died because of me." She forced back tears that threatened to weaken her. "You said my fate was tied with yours."

"I can only assume you betrayed me somehow, and that is the vision you saw. Do you seek to betray me?"

"Do you really think starting a war with the dark fae is wise?"

"I don't wish for war. I will take out the seeds of evil among my mother's people and give them peace."

"You expect them to accept the son of a light fae as their king? Your mere existence may very well be the cause for a war."

"That very reason has been why we have kept our secret." He twisted the stone that hung around his neck between his fingers. "But my mother's wishes change everything. Did you know she had a mate and a daughter?"

"No. I mean, I understood she had family but didn't know about them."

"Yes. They killed her mate along with her father. She sent her daughter, my half-sister, into hiding and I have reason to believe it was my sister who brought me this stone."

"I understand your desire to avenge them, but at least find out if any of this is true."

"You seem to know all about my past, how did you gain this information?"

"We have an excellent spymaster." How much did she share? She had placed herself in one hell of a predicament. Because she had stupidly bonded herself to Lucien, her loyalty was now torn between him and her king.

"What you have seen is not a certain future. I have learned that much from Storm, who has years of visions behind her. Matter of fact, she saw a dark beginning for you and I, but assured me if I chose the right path, things would work out."

"Right path? Great." For the first time in her life, Elaina didn't know where to turn or who to trust. The information she now held in the wrong hands would spell disaster. She understood Lucien's concerns. Felt his own turmoil as if it were her own. "Storm, does she know about your visitor?"

"I have told no one. Not even my brothers, as I was undecided on my decision. I think I should clue Storm in on all of this. She has been with us from the start and has wanted nothing more than to keep the peace."

She nodded. "I think maybe that's a good idea. We should do so right away." She stood, ready to march from his apartment when he took her hand into his.

"Elaina, we are mated now. There is no going back for either of us."

"Thanks to me." She let out a nervous laugh, but nothing about this was funny. "You should know that I am still loyal to Trevan and my people."

"I expect nothing less from you."

His words surprised her. "You would be okay if I turned you in?"

"You really think you could?"

"At this point, yes. Our bond is simply that, a bond."

"You belong to me now. No other can have you, Elaina." His eyes swirled with emotions she didn't even want to think about.

"Yes, I belong to you, but I do not love you. I love my people and my king and for them I would die."

Yet was what she said really true? Fae matings were as strong as any other immortal. To betray your mate would be the same as dying. She prayed she never had to test her resolve.

WHILE HE WASN'T SURPRISED AT HER WORDS AND LACK OF LOVE, IT still cut him worse than any blade ever could. Did he love her? He was certain he did. While she could care less about a mate, he had waited many years for her and had time for his love to grow. Even when he realized she belonged to him and the complications that came with it, his love was still there. He too was loyal, however, the thought of his sister out there living in fear for her life because of who she was did not bode well with him. Amber had not asked for her life either. She was also an innocent, same as he and his brothers.

"I am also loyal to those I care about and frankly tired of hiding what I am." He wasn't sure why he had said that, but it was true. "You are correct, your fate is tied to mine, but I would also die for my people."

"We seem to be at a stalemate," she replied.

"So, it would appear. Let us go seek Storm and her advice before we speak further of this." He walked to the door and held it open for her. They walked in silence, only greeting others as they passed them in the wide corridors of the palace. Lucien knew Storm was in her apartment, probably relaxing for the evening, and while he hated to disturb her, this was beyond important. When they reached her door, it swung open before he even knocked.

"I sensed you were coming." She looked at the two of them, then stepped aside. "Come in." She shut the door once they were inside.

"This conversation is going to require something stronger than coffee or tea, I assume?"

"It will," he replied.

She gave a nod. "Make yourselves comfortable. I'll pour the brandy."

Lucien placed his hand at the small of Elaina's back. The first touch since they had been so intimate and led her to the sofa where he waited for her to be seated before he sat next to her. She turned and gave him a scowl, but he ignored her. Storm came back with a tray holding three snifters of brandy and set them on the center table. Handing each of them a glass before taking a seat in the chair facing them.

"So, I sense you two are mated." Her brow jacked up to her hairline. "That was not something I was expecting so soon."

"Me neither," Elaina snapped back.

"It was not my doing." He tried to offer her his assurance, but right now his mate's emotions were on a rollercoaster ride.

Storm cleared her throat. "Okay. I think someone needs to start from the beginning."

"I'll go since it was me who tried to hide the mark on my wrist." Elaina launched into the story of when it first appeared, and since her motives were originally tied to trying to find out what Lucien was hiding, she retold her visit with Marcel.

"So, you were there at the ceremony?" Storm questioned.

"I was. Marcel gave me a cloaking stone and the spell to accompany it."

"I knew I sensed you there," he snarled.

"I assume you know everything now?" Storm leaned in, her body tense, waiting for a reply.

"I know who Lucien's parents were. Other than that, I'm not sure what else you guys are hiding." Elaina looked between Storm and him. Her gaze was full of worry. "This puts me in a position I don't really wish to be in."

Storm cast her gaze to the floor. "You're right, of course. Perhaps it's time I tell my brother the truth. I should prepare him should something happen."

"Something has happened," he added, then told her about the messenger, the stone and the note, which he had slipped into his pocket before leaving his apartment. He pulled the paper from his pocket and the stone from around his neck and handed both to her.

"I had Luna test the stone for me." He turned to Elaina. "Luna is blessed with a gift that allows her to hold an object and see who it belonged to and any history behind it."

He faced Storm again. "She confirmed it belongs to a dark fae royal and something that has passed from parent to child. She also saw the name Renna attached to it as well an amber which I think she mistook for the stone."

"How does an amber stone fit into this?" Elaina asked.

"Amber is my sister's name."

"Oh."

Storm stared at the stone, turning it in her fingers when Elaina interrupted.

"I think I had a vision. I saw Trevan dead and Lucien sitting on his throne." She retold the nightmare she had in gory detail, and hearing it again made the skin on the back of Lucien's neck crawl. He held zero desire to kill the king, even though he had threatened to do so if his mate kept fucking him. He no longer feared that. She was tied to him now, even if she didn't like it.

"So, this is why we came to you. Elaina fears whatever she does will bring about the death of her king and her people. I, on the other hand, am compelled to find my sister and at least find out what is going on with the dark fae."

"And if what Renna's note says is true? If the dark fae are in peril, as well as your sister, do you take back the throne?" Storm asked.

That was a question he couldn't answer. It was an impossible thing to choose between who lived and who died. "I do not know, but I can tell you that no matter what, if Amber is in danger, I will help her."

Storm gave a slight smile. "Then we have our answer. I'm afraid this is likely the darkness I saw for you, Lucien. Your mother was correct. Of the three of you, you have the darkest soul, but you also hold a kindness to you that overrules everything else. It is these two things that will guide you." She drew in a breath. "I suggest you try to track the messenger who I am willing to state was Amber herself. I will hold a private meeting with my brother and bring him up to speed."

"What about me? What should I do?"

"My dear niece, you will help your mate in any way you can. Between the two of you, you should be able to track this Amber down."

"I should be the one to tell Trevan of my mating."

Lucien growled. He hated the thought of his mate anywhere near the king.

"Suck it up, Lucien," Storm commanded. "Trevan is her king, and this is something she needs to do. Unless he releases her, she is still bound as his royal protector."

"My head knows this and, of course, you are correct." He faced Elaina. "You will do what you need to." Then she surprised him by touching his cheek.

"The day you first came to Drudora was the day I stopped having sexual relations with Trevan. I did not know why at the time, but now I do. Something inside me knew my mate was close." She smiled. "You need not worry. I may not be ready for this relationship, but I am faithful."

The words soothed his inner beast, and he kissed her palm. "Then go do what you must with my blessing."

CHAPTER 12

Elaina lay in her own bed, sleep a distant desire that she knew would never come to her. She'd sent Lucien back to his apartment after telling him she would go back to hers once she spoke to Storm. He'd gone, but his displeasure had filled the room and gave her a moment of pause, but she had stuck to her guns. Now alone in a bed that seemed ridiculously too large for her, she had second thoughts about everything. She brought her wrist up where she could see her mark and rubbed her thumb over the lines. She had asked Storm again if the dream she had might be a vision. It sure as hell felt real. Storm had thought it might be one of many possible futures and unfortunately, the ending was all up to choices that both Elaina and Lucien made. She had encouraged Elaina to nurture her new gift, and that was why she lay alone now.

Closing her eyes, she drew in a deep breath and let it out slowly. She repeated the process until calm came over her. Her mind was free of clutter as she floated to her favorite place. She stood with her face in the ocean breeze. The sun warmed her skin while the sound of the waves lulled her into a peaceful bliss.

"I was wondering if you might ever show up," a voice came from behind her, and she spun to face the female. There was no mistaking the jet-black hair that fell to her shoulders, wide blue eyes and pale creamy skin. The female was as tall as Elaina and dressed all in black, but that didn't hide the fact that she was underweight. The way she held herself, however, was that of one who had once been in royal court and in her gut she knew. This was a dark fae. This was Lucien's sister.

"Amber?"

"Elaina."

"Well, now, that we don't need introductions, how, and more importantly why, are you in my vision?"

"I would ask you the same, but I already know the answer." She looked around with a sad smile on her face. "I have been coming here since I was a child. It has been my only peace in life, and now you show up wearing my brother's mark. Sister."

Elaina blinked, as if that might help everything become clearer. "I've also been coming here." She looked at her mating mark. "Do you suppose this has caused us to see each other?"

"I do. We now share a link to my brother."

"Was it you who brought him the pendant?"

"Yes. Mother had given it to me the last time I saw her."

Suddenly, Elaina had a hunch. "You visited your mother in Hetus, didn't you?"

"Rarely, because she worried they might catch me, but yes." Tears streamed down the fae's cheek. "I would have killed them all for what they did to her and my family. I still intend to, but I cannot take them on alone."

"You realize that revealing the truth may start a war between all of us?"

Amber looked down at the sand. "Many may die, yes. But fewer will have to if we fight now. My cousin, the king, plans to invade your realm in three months' time. How many do you think will perish then?"

Her heart beat faster. "Amber, you need to tell us everything." The girl was fading. "Amber!"

"Come to New Orleans in the mortal realm. I will find you both there." Then she was gone.

Elaina bolted upright in her bed. Sweat beaded her forehead and chest as she tried to slow her racing heart. "Fuck!" What did she do now? She had planned to leave in the morning to see Trevan and tell him of her unplanned mating. Looking at the clock, it read 3:00 a.m. so she tossed the covers off and headed for the shower. Her plan was simple. By the time she was done showering, Trevan would be starting his day as he was an early riser. She'd see him first, then head back here to find Lucien and tell him of her encounter with Amber. It was imperative they find his sister, because that fae had information they desperately needed.

Inside the shower, she breathed a deep sigh and let the sweat of the night wash away. It was difficult to keep her mind from becoming a mess of emotions. She had to keep a clear head so she could analyze all the information handed to them. Lives depended on the choices she made. Choices Lucien made, and he was going to be hell bent on helping his sister. Could she blame him? Elaina hadn't been able to help her own sister—not that she had known Cassia was in trouble. But when she had finally learned that her sister had been in trouble, it was too late. Treason had been committed, and Elaina had done her duty and taken her sibling's head. The nightmare of the day would never leave her. Was she going to be forced to do the same with Lucien or those he loved? Would she be able to keep her king and her people safe? Deaths were coming. She felt it in her bones, and it caused a tear to slip down her cheek.

LUCIEN HAD BEEN RESTLESS ALL NIGHT AND HAD FINALLY GIVEN UP on sleep when he dressed and stood in front of the window overlooking the palace gardens. Gray clouds skated across the sky while rain pelted the ground, a perfect reflection of his mood. He wasn't happy his mate had stayed in her own bed, but it hadn't surprised him. Elaina needed time, and he had to give it to her no matter how much it tore him up inside.

As he stared into the rain-covered landscape, he felt a stir in his mind.

Lucien, can you hear me?

Elaina, I am surprised. Are you all right? He hadn't even tested their telepathic connection, wanting to give her time to adjust.

I am fine. Are you in your apartment still?

He smiled. *You should know exactly where I am.*

Seconds later, fae magic filled the air, followed by his mate who had jumped right into his living room. "This isn't normal, you know?"

"Then how did you know to reach out to me?"

"I recalled Harper saying something about telepathy with Roman, so I thought I'd give it a shot. Fae matings rarely bring about that type of connection. Granted, we can normally locate our mate and sense their emotions. Since we are both fae, I wasn't sure if it would work."

"Since all vampires have the ability, I assume it must be a dark fae thing."

She shrugged. "Perhaps."

"Did you speak to Trevan already?"

"Yes, and he was pleased for us."

He let out a dark laugh. "Until he finds out who I really am."

"About that. I had another vision last night."

He raised a brow and moved closer to her. "Was I sitting on his throne again?"

"No. I talked to Amber." She shifted her weight, a sign she was nervous. Not that he needed to see that, to know how she felt. Her emotions were part of him now.

"I think we might need to sit for this conversation." He waved his arm toward the sofa and was relieved when she moved to take a seat. He sat next to her, not willing to give her any more space. She'd had all night, after all.

"I have a place I like to go during meditation sometimes and... Well Amber showed up there and said we need to go to New Orleans, and she would find us there." She wrung her hands and her emotions bombarded him. Something was seriously bothering her, but he waited for her to finish. He took her hand in his and rubbed his thumb over hers. It seemed to help calm her.

"She said her cousin planned to invade in three months' time."

Now he understood the reason behind her turmoil. "Then I suggest we go immediately to New Orleans."

She nodded. "I agree." Then frowned. "You are fae, can't you jump?"

"I'm sure I can, but I have never done so. It would reveal too much and raise a lot of questions."

"That makes sense, but in this case, I think we need to move fast. I can take you with me." She stood, still holding his hand. "Are you ready?"

"Let's go."

Seconds later, they walked along a blaring Bourbon Street. It was evening in the mortal world and the air was thick with oppressing humidity, sweat and the stench of drunks. The partiers were many on both the sidewalk and street. To their right, a young mortal male threw up while his buddies cheered him on. Lucien simply shook his head, not understanding the appeal of such sport.

"I can't hear myself think," Elaina yelled over the music and shouts from humans who would question their life choices come morning. Before Lucien could respond, a female slipped in next to him and folded her arm around his.

"This way." She looked up at him for a moment, then focused her gaze straight ahead.

If he'd not known better, he would think Amber was wearing a costume. Her black hair was pulled into a high ponytail and her pointed ears not only exposed but covered with silver chains attached to small cuffs. She wore glitter on her lids that made her blue eyes pop, and her attire was nothing more than a piece of material that hardly covered her assets. What caused his gut to clench was she looked exactly like their mother and it brought back painful memories.

They made their way by weaving in and out of the crowd until Amber led them a few blocks away and to a shotgun home where she opened a wrought-iron gate and walked up to the front porch and unlocked the door, allowing them to enter first. Once inside, she closed the door and walked from the front parlor further back to the kitchen.

"You guys want something?"

"Information," he replied, taking a seat on a stool at the granite counter.

She grabbed a bottle of water from the fridge and downed nearly half of it before wiping her mouth. "Sorry. I hate the weather here, but New Orleans is a great place to hide. I blend in as a waitress slash bartender and everyone thinks my ears are cool."

"And I'm certain they think the rest of your skimpy outfit is cool as well." He allowed the snarl in his tone to come through.

"Hey, you don't get to play brother just yet."

"Why not use glamour to hide yourself?" Elaina asked, taking a seat next to Lucien.

Amber laughed. "I use as little magic as possible. Every time I do, the threat of being found goes up. I've managed to blend in here for the past ten years."

"Understandable. So, you pass yourself off as human?" He didn't like the fact that his sister had to work to keep food on her table. She was a princess, after all.

"I have for many years. I move to another part of the world until people become suspicious, then change my name and move again." She leaned on the counter. "But you are going to change all of this for me. For all of us."

He shook his head. "I need more to go on."

Elaina interrupted. "You told me your cousin was planning an invasion?"

"Yes. Even though I don't live in my home of Claromond, I still have a few allies who risk their lives to keep me informed."

"Tell us everything," Lucien insisted.

Amber gave a nod, then began. "When I was five, my uncle, with the help of my cousin, killed my father and grandfather while they were out on a hunting trip. A member of the hunting party got away and back to the palace to warn my mother. She sent me off with the nanny into the mortal realm and I never saw my home again." She bit her lip and swallowed. Lucien wanted to go to her, but felt she needed to do this on her own.

"Word reached us that mother was auctioned off as a slave and Glenna—she was my nanny—learned that a light fae had been the one to purchase mother. Eventually, we found out it was Micah, and I went in search of her. When I finally located her, she was already heavy with your eldest brother. Micah kept mother's magic bound, so she could not escape, and I wasn't strong enough yet to help her. By the time I was, the three of you were already teens and mother was certain that her second-born son would be the salvation for the dark fae. She begged me to wait until the time was right, then come to you for help."

"How were you even able to enter Hetus with no one being the wiser?" Elaina asked. "Your presence would have been felt all the way to Drudora."

"I did what I had to. I took the form of a light fae."

His mate stiffened beside him. "You took an innocent life so you could transform into someone else?"

Amber glared at Elaina, her gaze ice cold. "I did what I had to in order to survive and seek the only family I had left." She looked away and back at Lucien. "I only killed twice. After that I made a sacrifice in order to gain enough power to glamour myself against detection."

Lucien's back went rigid. To glamour against detection from mortals was far easier than doing so in a territory filled with fae. What had his sister given for such power? He would not force the issue. If she wanted to share, then she would do so. "Please, continue."

Realizing he would not judge her, she began again. "Since mother was resigned to her fate, I vowed to kill her tormentor, and that is exactly what I did. I poisoned Micah and left mother a dagger at her request. I promised her I would deliver the package to you when I felt the time was right and now here you are."

"You killed Micah?"

Amber straightened and flashed him a look of defiance, lifting her chin. "I did and would do it a thousand times over if I had the power to do so."

He smiled. "Sister, you did us all a favor and for that I thank you."

"Did your mother ever tell you why Micah bought her then forced her to bear him children?" Elaina tapped the counter to bring attention to her question.

"He thought his sons would one day help him take back Drudora." She laughed. "Little did he know that his life would end before he could bring his wishes into play."

"It's as if Micah had two sides to him," Elaina whispered.

"Indeed. However, if you analyze his every move, everything was done to protect himself. Changing the DNA of Jarrah's creations stopped the killing of the fae in Hetus. They revered him. I'm still not sure I understand why he took my mother."

"I think I might," Elaina blurted out. "Renna owed Jarrah a favor and gave him her blood. He used that, mixed with his own, and that is how he created the vampires he unleashed on his brother."

Amber and Lucien stared at her.

"What favor could my mother have possibly owed a light fae?" Lucien asked.

"We will probably never know, but it is written in our books how Jarrah did it."

"And Micah knew this so, to get back at his brother, he took the woman responsible for helping to create the vampires. Forced her to bear his sons and then he planned to use us at some point, but both brothers died before the plan could be unleashed." Lucien grimaced when he looked at his sister, who held a small grin.

"You can thank me for Jarrah's death as well. He blackmailed my mother for her blood. It seems many years ago, there was a brief peace between our people. My mother was a young princess and at her father's urging she attended court in Drudora to meet with Jarrah and Micah."

"This must have been before the fight between the brothers," Elaina commented.

Amber nodded in agreement. "Yes, and Jarrah made advances that my mother tried to ignore. Seemed he didn't like the fact she didn't want to sleep with the king of Drudora so one night he went into her chambers and raped her. He then told her if she ever spoke of it, he would tell her betrothed it was she who crawled into his bed that night and what was he to do, after all? Mother knew that all she had to do was go to either her father or her betrothed and they would believe her, but she also knew it would start a war and many fae would die. She kept Jarrah's dirty little secret, and that was how he gained her blood." Amber slammed her fists on the counter. "It was Jarrah who helped my uncle and cousin take the throne. While he never told my grandfather, I later learned that he whispered that my mother was a whore and I a bastard child. It was enough for my cousin and uncle to start a war. They were more than happy to sell my mother to Micah and kill my family. I would be dead too, if not for my mother. I am still being hunted."

Lucien's jaw tightened so hard he feared cracking every tooth. He bared his fangs in a hiss of anger. Two brothers. Two light fae had hurt his mother. Used her body against her will. Something dark inside him snapped, and he spoke with a growl.

"I will take back what belongs to my family and restore your honor."

CHAPTER 13

Elaina's stomach dropped when Lucien uttered his vow. "Lucien, your dark fae is showing."

"So it is, and so it shall. I'm done hiding who I am because of two selfish bastard brothers. They have destroyed so many lives and it's time to end their terror."

The darkness inside him became a living thing that Elaina felt brush across her skin, and it frightened her. Was the vision she had seen of her slain king about to become reality? Not knowing what else to do, she laid her hand on his arm and immediately he relaxed under her touch. Perhaps this mating thing was going to come in handy.

"Lucien. I know you are angry, and you have every right to be. Your mother and sister have been treated poorly and deserve to be avenged. Unfortunately, the men who were responsible are dead and you cannot kill them again." She looked at Amber. "Your sister seems to have some inside information. If her cousin really is planning to invade us, then we need to know everything she does and work on a plan." He softened further under her fingers and she sighed with relief.

"You are right, of course. Amber, what else can you tell us about your world?"

"Our people are in anguish. They would fight back if they thought they could win, but the current crown and his army keep a tight grip on everyone. If even a whisper of a revolution is heard, they publicly execute the culprits along with their family. My cousin spares no one."

Lucien reached for Elaina's hand and she allowed him to thread his fingers between hers, knowing he needed her to center him.

"Have you any idea how many supporters he has?" Elaina asked.

"No, but I think he is hanging on by a thread." She reached across the counter and touched her brother's arm. "If he comes after King Trevan and the others, he will force our people to follow him and do his bidding. Many will perish. But, if we strike first, we will have the upper hand. He will not expect it for one, and once our people see a chance at freedom, they will support you." She chewed her lip. "Rumors are that I still live and will one day come back to free them. It is what gives them hope, but I am not their true leader. You are. You have already ruled in your brother's place and this is your destiny."

"You are the eldest, you are rightfully their queen."

She shook her head. "No, brother. Our world does not rule by the eldest child, it is the one who holds the crown and that is you. Mother chose you." Her gaze dropped to the pendant around his neck. "Break the stone and hold the crown."

Elaina and Lucien both stared at her. "What?" he asked.

"The crown. Once you break the stone, the crown becomes yours and all will see that you are the rightful king."

"You mean he literally breaks the stone and holds the crown to Claromond?"

Amber straightened and looked at them as if they were both daft. "Yes. The crown attached to the stone is Lucien's and will go to him once he shatters the crystal. When my grandfather was slain, the crown vanished, as is customary. Normally, it would have gone to my mother because she held the stone as chosen by her father, but... Well, we know what happened there. A jealous sibling."

Lucien picked up the stone and held it where he could better inspect it. "I would never have thought this was the real crown of the dark fae. If I shatter the stone, then how will it pass on to the next king or queen?"

"Once you are on the throne, the demon will repair the stone and give it back to you. You know, the demon you summon now to hide your power."

"The demon who takes pieces of my soul?"

"He does not take your soul. He takes your darkness but because it is part of you, it feels like your soul."

"Who is this demon?" Lucien asked.

"He is Vezrath, our god."

Lucien pressed his palm to his forehead and closed his eyes. "I had no idea we were summoning a god. A demon god, no less."

"Things just get insaner by the second," she whispered. "So, this tiny crown is the real deal."

Amber flashed a determined glare at them. "It is the true crown of the *nqcao aran plural erain or rein.*"

"The falcon king," Elaina whispered. She looked at Lucien and their gazes met. In a flash, she was somewhere else.

Blood pooled the stone floor as Elaina walked the palace corridors. Except this place she did not recognize. It was not the palace of Drudora or Glenmoore. Voices and laughter filled the air, and she hurried to follow it. In the throne room, she saw a group of men drinking a toast. One was Lucien and he wore a crown just like the one attached to his stone. Next to him stood Trevan, and Lucien's brothers Andrei and Dorin. When Lucien spotted her, his eyes warmed with love and he smiled.

"My queen." He held out his hand. "Come and celebrate with us."

"Elaina?"

She gasped and was jerked back to reality.

"Elaina? Are you okay? You went somewhere else for a bit." Lucien held concern in his eyes, and she felt him probe her mind to seek reassurance she was indeed fine.

"I think I just had a vision. You were the king of Claromond and this time Trevan was standing beside you along with your brothers. You were laughing and drinking."

He palmed her cheek. "How do we make that vision our reality and not the one where your king lay dead?"

"I... I believe you must make the first move. We should see if Storm has spoken to Trevan."

He nodded. "I agree. We need to go to my brothers in Hetus and call for Storm and Trevan to meet with us." He looked at Amber. "You will come with us and meet Andrei and Dorin. Andrei will want you under his protection."

"It would honor me to meet my other brothers face to face."

"Good. Then let us be gone."

※

Lucien wasn't able to stand still while Amber and Elaina retold everything they knew so far. Every so often, Andrei would look up and check on him as Lucien paced the room and sucked back a whiskey. Everyone seemed to take the story in stride, and probably better than he was. How had his life gone from mundane to full throttle in a matter of days? He had a mate and still didn't even know how to handle that situation, considering Elaina hadn't consented. While most might say cross that bridge later, he felt it was far too important to wait. It was something that had to be addressed as soon as possible. He stopped and took a moment to watch her. His beautiful warrior fae mate. She was in her element when it came to planning a coup, as that seemed to be exactly what they were doing. Then he looked at his sister. He had thought his life had been cursed, but hers had been far worse. To run for your life and hide—well he understood the hiding part—wasn't a way to live. Both women needed his protection, like it or not.

"We can't go marching in there with an army. If my cousin gets word that you are coming, who knows what he may do." Amber's gaze went to each person at the table, then up to Lucien. "We have to slip into the palace and kill him. Take the throne quietly, then bring in your warriors to finish off any of his followers. My people will not have any qualms in turning in the traitors."

"You say you have a contact?" Trevan asked.

"Yes. My mother's youngest brother, who has managed to stay under the radar. He works in the king's guard and no one knows his true identity. He is familiar with the layout as well as the king's routine."

"That's a valuable person to have on the inside, but are you certain we can trust him, and this isn't a trap?" Lucien asked. "I mean, it is his own nephew on the throne right now. How is it that the king doesn't recognize his own uncle?"

"Aven was away for many years prior to and during the slaughter. Some friends warned him before he came back, so he was prepared. He made a deal with Vezrath, the demon god, who somehow hides his true identity."

Lucien then turned to Elaina. "And this spymaster of yours who has a contact in the dark fae realm? Who might that be?"

"I am not sure as he didn't reveal that to me."

"I will find that out," Trevan said. "Though my spymaster is quite skilled, there is the possibility that a dark fae spy who is laying a trap has taken him in."

"Or," Lucien interjected, "is it Aven who is feeding your spymaster information?"

Amber looked up at him, confusion in her eyes. "Why would he give our enemy information that might destroy us?"

"Was that his intention?" Sonia, who had been quiet this entire time, finally spoke up and everyone looked at Andrei's mate, the queen of Hetus. She explained. "Things are desperate for the dark fae, and what better way to gain help than from your oldest enemy?" She shook her head. "It seems obvious to me that this cousin is not only a threat to the dark fae, but everyone. I would seek help anywhere I could find it. Including from my enemy."

"This makes sense." Trevan smiled. "Andrei, your mate is a very smart woman, as I would likely do the same."

Andrei beamed with pride. "She is very astute, and I am a lucky man." He looked back at everyone else. "I too would likely seek help anywhere I could get it if I thought it would help my people."

"Then here is the plan I propose," Elaina said. "Trevan will speak with his spymaster and gather any information he can. I think Roman and myself should try to enter Claromond and get the lay of the land."

"Wait, you and Roman?" Lucien questioned.

"It makes sense since we are both royal protectors," Roman said from across the room where he sat next to his mate, Princess Harper.

"It will be us that lead the warriors into battle and any information we can gain will potentially save lives."

Lucien stood, stance wide and arms crossed over his chest. "My mate will not waltz right into enemy hands," he snarled. The glare Elaina threw his way should have been enough to make any man back down, but he wasn't any man. He was a dark fae prince and would be damned if his mate was going to try to pull this stunt on him.

"It is my duty, as you very well know," she shot back.

He stood his ground and shook his head. "Not without me."

Amber moved beside him and touched his arm. "He is not wrong in his request. You would likely be caught, and the king would enjoy executing you for all to see. Even if he didn't detect you right away, any of the fae there would turn you in to gain the king's favor."

"Then what do you propose we do?" Elaina matched his stance. His mate was defiant, but then he already knew that.

"Only a royal dark fae will be able to enter without detection." Amber looked to Lucien. "I will take you, Andrei and Dorin. You will have to slay the king while he sleeps."

"Andrei stays. He is too important to his people," he said.

"While I'm glad you worry about me, brother—" Andrei rose from his seat next to Sonia. "I stand by you. Therefore, I will be going. You may be the chosen king of Claromond, but both Dorin and I are a dark fae prince. Renna was my mother as well as yours and I will see her avenged." He looked down at his mate. "Sonia is the queen of Hetus. Should I die in battle, she will take my place."

The fear his sister-in-law held back was not lost on Lucien as she reached up and squeezed her mate's hand in a show of support.

"Then it is settled," Amber spoke. "Tonight, Lucien will break the stone and claim his crown and get the blessing from Vezrath before we head into Claromond."

CHAPTER 14

Lucien was back in his apartment until he would meet with his brothers and sister in the same location they used to perform the full moon ritual. He still had a lot of questions as he gathered his favorite blades, but they would have to wait. A knock at his door had him wondering why his mate didn't simply enter. Moving to open it, he waved her inside.

"You are my mate. My place is your place." He wasn't even going to venture into the realm of where the two of them would live. He knew the choices for her would not be easy. First things first. He had a bastard king to kill.

"I'm going with you to the ritual."

He lifted his gaze from the blade he was wiping down. "I see."

"That's it?"

"Did you expect me to deny you?" He raised a brow.

"I did, actually." She looked at the marking on her wrist. "I should also go with you to Claromond. As your mate, it is my right."

"You are a light fae and will be detected."

"We don't know what I am for certain. Would it stand to reason that I might have changed?"

He thought for a moment. "There is the possibility. It seems mates share traits. Roman took on fae when he mated Harper, but you and I are in uncharted territory."

"But you also carry the blood of my people and that concerned me, so I questioned your sister."

Again, he arched a brow. "You have concern for me?"

She crossed her arms. "Don't be absurd. Of course, I have concerns. Just because I mistakenly bonded us, doesn't mean I don't feel the bond and worry for your safety."

He chuckled. "Of course."

Her gaze narrowed. "What is so amusing?"

He put his dagger on the kitchen table and motioned for her to have a seat as he pulled out his own chair. He would have offered to pull it out for her, but she would have shoved him out of her way. His mate was very independent.

"You have made it clear how you feel about me, but now let me make myself clear." He clasped his hands together on the table. "I have been waiting for you my entire life. Wondering when the day might arrive when I would see your face. I have had centuries to fall in love with my mate."

"What?" She blinked as if that might help her understand his words better.

"I love you." He shook his head. "But I think you already know that since you can feel my emotions and that scares you most."

She offered a nervous laugh. "Why would your feelings frighten me?"

"Because you want no one to see you vulnerable. I see you, *dragoste*. I see the hard, determined warrior who would willingly lay down her life to protect those she cares about. I also see the kind, soft female who hates killing. The one who craves for someone to see the real her. Well, here I am. I see you and love all of you."

She cast her gaze to the table, unable to look at him. "I had no idea you saw right through me like that."

"Your vulnerabilities are nothing to be ashamed of. They are what make you the passionate woman that you are."

"This whole mating thing seems to be better suited to you than it is me. I am clueless, as you already know, due to the fact I bound us together. That was an obvious amateur move."

"Neither of us knew it would happen so quickly. Perhaps fate thought we needed a push."

She looked back at him. "Perhaps, but unlike you, I cannot confess love."

"You keep yourself closed off to all my feelings so all you have right now is what the bond gives you. Nothing more than a need to protect me." He let out a sigh. "I will not force you into anything you are not ready for. Once I take the throne, I would have you by my side as my queen should you choose to be there."

"And if I don't choose it?"

"Then you may continue on with your life as is." Not wanting to deepen this discussion further, because he wasn't sure how he'd let her go if that was indeed what she chose, he changed the subject. "You said earlier that you questioned Amber? What did you learn?"

"I was first curious why you and your brothers present as vampire—the fangs and need for blood. I understand that dark fae only drink blood if they wish to take on another form." She sucked in a breath. "Seems I was way off base and there is so much we do not know about dark fae."

"Please continue."

"Dark fae don't drink blood, only the royalty do. When Vezrath created the dark fae, he made them in his image. Well, somewhat anyway. The royalty require blood in order to survive, which explains the fangs. He gifted your ancestors with two animal spirits and immense powers. The general population of dark fae do not drink blood and hold no spirit animal. If they choose to take on another human-like form, they must kill the person, fae, whoever, to do so."

He rubbed at the scruff on his chin. "So, most everything we knew about dark fae is actually untrue."

She nodded. "Well, we didn't know much, but yes. Your people seem to like to keep their secrets to themselves."

"As do the light fae."

"Indeed."

"If this were true though, then why did Amber mention killing to steal a form? Should she not also have an animal spirit?" None of this made any sense to him since she was a full blood dark fae royal.

"Because she was so young when she left her mother, she didn't have the ability until much later in life and she had to figure it out on her own."

"Makes sense." There was still worry in her eyes so he continued. "What else?"

"Amber believes that when you seek Vezrath tonight, you will lose your light fae DNA."

"Why?"

"She thinks it will be the sacrifice he requests to grant you the crown, plus it might be the only way to gain your full power. The king must be a dark fae."

"And this has you worried?"

"My vision. It might explain why you sat on Trevan's throne with his blood at your feet."

"You think if I turn completely, I will fulfill your vision."

"And worse," she whispered.

ELAINA WASN'T SURE WHAT SHE HOPED FOR. IF LUCIEN DIDN'T KILL the king and take his place on the throne, the current king of Claromond was going to invade so war was still a real possibility. Damn, she wished she knew what to do. Was letting Lucien take the throne and become a dark fae the right path? So many pieces of the puzzle were missing. What part did she play? She must have some kind of role in this considering they were mated. Fate had chosen them for a reason, and she had to believe it had something to do with his destiny. It hadn't been lost on her how she could calm him. Sooth the darkness inside him when it flared to life. Was that why she'd been chosen?

"You are lost in thought. Tell me, what do you think I should do?"

She snapped out of her thoughts and looked at Lucien. "I wish I knew. I believe one choice will lead to my king's death along with my people. The other might be their salvation, but which one?"

He stepped closer, touched her shoulders and gazed into her eyes.

"My heart tells me I am on the correct path. That taking my rightful place will bring peace. Who better to lead the dark fae than a half-breed king and his light fae mate?" He smiled. "This is what I need to do."

"Then allow me to go with you to Claromond." She hated staying behind.

"Your place is with your king. Besides, I cannot concentrate on the task at hand and worry about you at the same time." He cupped her face, and that was when she felt it. The warm embrace of his feelings for her wrapped around her and hugged her in its embrace. It was so much more than she ever expected, and her eyes filled with unshed tears. No one had ever loved her like this. Not even her sister, and her parents had only come slightly closer, and they had adored her. This was a love that stole her breath and she understood why he asked her to stay safe. It was hard to believe that this man standing in front of her was full of so much emotion for her. He was a male full of darkness. A predator who wasn't afraid of anything except of losing her.

"I will stay here and wait for your word." She hated giving in but realized perhaps it was for the best. Maybe this was the role she played. Perhaps it was his feelings for her that would keep him centered. She was going to lay a lot of lives on this one hope.

"It's time for us to go." He kissed her forehead. Then the tip of her nose before claiming her mouth. His kiss deepened and was full of desperation. Full of a man who held a fear he may never see her again, and for the first time in her life, she wanted to open fully to someone. Allow him to see inside to all of her. Lucien was an enigma she didn't even pretend to understand. She had thought she both feared and hated him for what he was. Now, she realized the emotion was only fear. He was not responsible for the past. He was simply another pawn in a war between brothers, and now he was going to make the best of everything the only way he knew how. Her fear of him was borne out of the way he made her feel. That he made her feel at all. He alone had caused her to reexamine everything she knew and felt.

Did she love him? She wasn't sure what love was other than how she had felt for her family. She had loved them. What she experienced in this moment was so much stronger than that small emotion from her past. That he may turn into something dark and sinister left her distressed. The fact he may not come back at all? Well, she refused to even acknowledge it was a possibility because of the pit it left in her stomach. She may not say she loved him, but she was positive life without him in it wasn't an option any longer.

How she had come so far in such a short time left her baffled.

When he ended the kiss and moved away from her, she was cold but shoved back a shiver. Instead, she took his hand and looked him square in the eyes.

"Promise you will come back alive and whole."

"I wish for no other outcome than to have you in my arms again. But, if I fail, then you must prepare yourself and Trevan the best you can. If you have to flee into hiding, then do it."

All she could do was nod and hold on to the thought that this was going to work. Together, they made the jump back to the mountains where the next chapter of their lives was about to begin. Dorin and Amber stood talking next to the fire, while Andrei and his mate Sonia held each other in the shadows. Elaina had a grave understanding of the emotions the vampire queen was experiencing.

Out of the darkness, Trevan appeared and next to him stood a man Elaina had not seen in so many years she thought he might be dead.

"Olarhan," she whispered.

"Who?" Lucien asked, and of course, it was unlikely he would have ever heard of the Falock.

"Olarhan is what we refer to as a Falock. His mother was fae and his father a powerful warlock. He's at least three thousand years old that we know of, maybe more. I thought him dead since we have not seen him in my lifetime." She stared at the tall, lean man with white hair that fell to his waist. He had the ears of his fae mother and the deep green eyes of his warlock father. It was rumored his power was immense, but Elaina had to wonder what he was doing here and with Trevan? How had Trevan even found him?

"Everyone," Trevan called out as he approached. "I wanted to come and assure you that our people now have the protection of Olarhan." He smiled. "I know many of you have never heard of him, but he is a powerful fae warlock. He was a favorite of my mother and as her wish would have been our safety, he will see us to his realm while we wait this out."

"Everyone?" Storm asked.

"All territories that wish to go. Dark fae blood cannot cross to my home so you will be safe there."

Elaina didn't miss the message that was loud and clear. The brothers could not cross, and neither could Amber, but what about her? Did she now hold any dark fae blood because of Lucien? He must have been thinking the same thing because he looked at her, panic in his eyes.

"I will come for you, but if I am unable, hide in the human realm. I will find you no matter what."

Olarhan approached them before she could say more and stopped in front of Lucien. His frame towered a good four inches over the vampire. Power filled the air until she thought she might choke on it.

"Dark vampire," he snarled. "I have little use for your kind, but I will offer you this. Blood will spill because of you, so choose your path wisely. Don't believe what you see to be true. You have the power to change reality but understand that the demon will extract his price." He then jerked his head at Elaina. "She is not welcome in my world. Her blood is tainted." He looked at Andrei and Sonia. "Same with her so be sure you come back alive with victory on your heels, or they may both end up dead."

Then he vanished.

"I have every faith that you will succeed, but I will stay behind and protect the women," Trevan said.

"No!" Elaina yelled. Was this how the vision of her king dead came to fruition? She would make certain, somehow, he didn't stay behind.

CHAPTER 15

The weight of two worlds was heavy on his shoulders, and for a moment, he wondered if he really could succeed. He had little choice, and he certainly had to come back alive or his mate, along with his sister-in-law, might perish. As he, his two brothers and his sister approached the fire, he had to put everything else behind him. He owed his mother his life and his people their freedom. It was time to bring the dark fae into the light.

While his siblings began the chant that would call forth Vezrath, he pulled the leather cord that held the stone from around his neck and palmed it. With a squeeze, he crushed the stone in his hand and held his breath.

The fire burned hotter and higher until flames reached twenty feet in the air. When Lucien opened his palm, the shattered crystal lay in his pooled blood. The blood dripped to the ground, staining the snow red, and that was when the black smoke thickened and took the shape of the demon. The demon spoke, his voice a low, thick slice of Hell.

"You summon me to ask for the crown? Are you prepared to embrace your darkness?" His red eyes were pinned on Lucien.

There was no hesitation. "Yes."

Vezrath laughed. "We shall see." Then he walked from the fire. His body, a wide, muscular, black-skinned, ten feet of lethal demon. Vezrath's fangs extended as he made his way toward Lucien. Tension from all the onlookers thickened the air as they waited to see what happened next.

The demon stopped and stared down at him, forcing Lucien to tip his head back to meet Vezrath's gaze head on. He squared his shoulders, and the demon laughed again.

"You have guts, I'll give you that." Then without warning, Vezrath slammed his fist into Lucien's chest and grabbed his heart.

In the distance, he heard Elaina scream, but he couldn't move. His feet frozen in place and not even his lungs could move to suck in air. This was how he was going to die. A demon god was going to rip his heart out before he even got the chance to earn that crown. A buzzing filled his head, and he realized Vezrath was in his mind rooting around. Was his heart not enough? Now, the demon wanted to split his brain open from the inside.

Fucker.

He was not giving in to the white-hot searing pain that threatened to take him to his knees. His veins filled with fire and soon his bones were going to turn to ash. Yet, he never broke his gaze or flinched. Instead, he unlocked his jaw and forced words past his lips.

"That all you got?"

The demon offered a maniacal laugh, brought his head closer and replied, "No." Then let loose such blackness and horror that Lucien questioned why he had taunted the demon god in the first place. This time he actually prayed for death, and quickly. When he thought his sweat-soaked body could take no more, Vezrath retracted his clawed hand and released not only his heart, but the grip on his mind. He then shoved his other wrist into Lucien's face.

"Drink."

Stunned he had the strength to do so, he struck quickly through the thick leathery skin until he hit pay dirt. The first pull of blood surprised him and was not what he expected. The demon's blood was sweet, and he took several more pulls until forced to stop.

"Enough!" Vezrath jerked free, blood still dripping from his wrist, and Lucien's gaze focused on it. He wanted more, for now he tasted the power, the precious life force carried with it. It was filled with dark, raw magic that called to him. He was drawn away when the demon spoke again, and he noticed Vezrath held the crown between his hands.

"Lucien, son of Renna, your blood now runs black, and you are the chosen to hold the throne." He placed the crown on Lucien's head then produced a knife with a twelve-inch blade. The handle was simple and wrapped in leather and the blade glistened in the firelight, but Lucien instinctively knew this was a special weapon. Vezrath handed him the blade, then spoke. "Rule well." Then he was gone, and the fire died back down to its normal size.

He rolled his fingers into his palms and closed his eyes. So much darkness swirled inside him, he no longer felt like himself. Evil surged through him and whispered temptations in his ear. As suddenly as his urges to lash out and rip apart anything that stood in his way came over him, they disappeared. When his head cleared, he realized Elaina was next to him, her hand on his arm.

"How do you feel? You look different."

"Different how?"

"More like a dark fae. Your hair is darker and your eyes… They seem to switch from blue to brown like they can't decide what color to be."

He looked at her and full understanding of how important she was to him centered him. She was the light that was going to keep this darkness in check.

"I feel like part of me is gone." Then he pulled her to him, needing to feel her softness pressed against his hard edges. He breathed in her scent and never wanted to let go of her. Yet, he knew he had to. There was no stopping the events that were put into motion. He was now the rightful king to the dark fae, and his duty was to take back what someone had ripped from his family. Still, he had one last need before he stepped into the other side. He bent to her ear.

"I need you."

She seemed to understand what he couldn't find the words to convey and looked over his shoulder at the others. "We need some time. Lucien will call for you when he is ready." And without another word, she flashed them both back to his apartment.

His desires took on a life of their own and as soon as they were in his living room, he reached for the neck of her tee and tore it from her body. "I am going to fuck you. Hard."

She responded by reaching for his own shirt, which she had removed in seconds, then started on his jeans but fumbled with the button. He jerked her hands away. "Strip," he commanded, and she dared not disobey.

While she peeled off her pants, he undressed and began palming his erection. So much need built up inside of him he could hardly think straight. He lifted her off her feet and wrapped her thighs around his waist. In a single thrust, he was deep inside her. Planted balls deep, and yet it still wasn't enough. He spun and walked until her back smacked against the door, as that was the closest vertical surface to where they started. Planting his palms on either side of her, his body kept her locked in place. He sucked a nipple in his mouth and flicked his tongue until the bud couldn't tighten any further.

She moaned, and it only served to fuel the darkness inside him that would take what belonged to him.

Her.

He would take all of her and hope it served to keep him sane while he was gone. Moving his hips, he didn't slow but pistoned in and out of her. "You are mine, now and forever. My brand on your wrist is not enough," he whispered in her ear. "I will mark every inch of your body, so you never forget who I am." He struck fast and hard. His fangs piercing the flesh at her neck and he drank.

She screamed. Her nails dug into his back, but he never relented. He only grew harder as her core spasmed around his cock and coated him with her orgasm. Releasing his fangs, he moved to her other nipple and pierced right through the center and she thanked him by coming again. Yet he still wasn't done. This time he bit the swell of her breast and she came yet again. With every sip of blood, his world righted a little more. Finally, he growled out as his own orgasm took hold of him and sent him over the edge. Slowly, he moved inside her and retracted his fangs. He moved his arms around her to cushion her back from the door, cursing at himself for being so brutal. She was going to hate him for his next move, but it was vital, or he might change his mind about everything. He could forget the world outside existed when he was inside her.

Kissing her, he memorized her taste. Her smell, her feel until she would forever be in his memories, then he pulled free and gently set her to her feet. He bent and kissed her cheek. "Forgive me for this and what I am about to do but remember that I love you." Then he jumped from her life.

HER BRAIN HARDLY HAD TIME TO REGISTER THAT HE HAD LEFT. Elaina stood naked and cold, and she knew deep inside her he was telling her goodbye in case he never came back.

"You bastard," she cried out and tears slipped from her eyes. Elaina wasn't one to cry, but there was no stopping this. She allowed herself to slip to the floor and have this one moment of weakness before she had to warrior up.

I love you too. I hope you can hear me.

There was no reply, and she really did not know if he received her words or not. She prayed he had because she needed him to know this and fight like hell to come back. She looked at her mark and touched it with her fingertips. It was neither hot nor cold. It simply was, and in this moment, she had never felt more alone. Wiping away her tears, she stood and remembered she was fae. Not just any fae, but a royal protector and now the mate of a dark fae king. She had shit to do, so she jumped to her own apartment to take a quick shower and dress.

Twenty minutes later. She located her king and stood in front of him.

"Evacuation has already begun," Trevan announced. "Storm and the people in her territory are already gone since they were the smallest. Plus, she is helping everyone get settled on the other side."

"What about Hetus?"

"Sonia is helping them right now, and both Roman and Harper are here in Drudora getting our people out. We expect everyone to be gone in the next twenty minutes."

"And when will you be going?" She offered him her most stern look.

"I should stay here."

"No, you should not. You are the only leader our people have Sonia and I will be fine. I will see to her safety. By the way, what have you told our people?"

He grimaced. "The truth as is owed them." Sighing, he continued. "You are right, but at least allow me to leave you some guards."

"I will be staying," a deep voice called out, and when they looked, they saw Roman approaching. Not only was he Trevan's son-in-law, but he was also a royal guard to Andrei and had been around for a few thousand years as one of the original vampires.

"My daughter must be beside herself," Trevan replied.

"She is not happy about it but understands my duty to my queen. I am bound to protect her by the blood of your uncle until such time as I am released from my bond." He lifted his chin and crossed his arms. "I have no desire for release."

The king's relief was notable. "I am glad for your duty then. You will come to us the moment this is over?"

Since out of the three of them staying behind, Roman was the only one allowed to cross into the Falock's realm, it made sense that he could sound the return home. Providing they had a home left to return to.

"Harper and I can reach each other telepathically. We have already tested our link, and it works thanks to Olarhan leaving a tiny opening in his veil."

Those words gave Elaina a little hope. Maybe the unbearable silence she experienced was because the veil between their realm and Claromond was so secure even their link to each other couldn't get through. She had to believe that Lucien would reach out to her if he was able.

"The last of Hetus's people have gone through the veil, all that are left are Cristian and Taos, who will watch over Sonia. I suggest you and I go there now. It's time for Trevan to leave as well," Roman said as he pointed at two fae warriors who stood outside the door waiting to escort the king.

Trevan stepped into Elaina's space. "I'm sure your mate will be successful and soon we will all be back and can mend relations between us and our dark brothers and sisters."

She gave a nod. "I hope you are right, but this feeling of doom inside of me isn't going to subside until this is over and my mate is back here safe and sound." This was maybe the first time she had openly called Lucien her mate, and it didn't feel foreign to her. How had things changed so quickly she wondered as she watched her king walk away with his guards?

"He's right, you know?" Roman pulled her from the dark thoughts that kept tumbling around in her head.

"That Lucien will be successful?" She eyed the vampire—now also half fae, thanks to his mate—with suspicion. The last time the two of them had exchanged words was when he had come to Trevan's court, and Elaina had been anything but trusting of him.

"I've known him for many years. He is a powerful vampire and I suspect he's even more so now."

Elaina realized that she probably had the only other vampire standing in front of her that not only knew Lucien best, but he was also familiar with a fae mating a dark and deadly man.

His brow jacked up. "I suspect you have questions. I will do my best to answer once we are back in Hetus."

They moved outside to speak to the last of her warriors before they made the jump. "I'm surprised you would be so forthcoming after the way I treated you."

He grinned. "All is forgiven, but you ever do that again and I will drag you into the ring for a sparring match."

She laughed, some of the tension rolling off her. "I would gladly accept that match." Something told her that this royal guard might actually have a thing or two he could teach her.

CHAPTER 16

Lucien hated the way he'd left Elaina, but her words of love were the last thing he heard before he shut her out completely and it had touched him deeply. He knew he should remain open to her, but to do so would be a costly mistake. She was a distraction that would cause him to falter at precisely the wrong moment and cost lives. Maybe even his own. He had to succeed, if for nothing else than her safety.

He stood with his brothers and sister on the outskirts of some hick town in the human realm. Amber had said this location had a minor breach in the veil thanks to her uncle and would be easier to enter Claromond undetected. They might be dark fae, but there was still a chance the king might notice a change in his territory. He was edgy, but not for the reason one would expect. The power that coursed through him was immense, and that had been why he had taken Elaina hard and fast. She grounded him. Soothed the power inside him so he could think more clearly. He pulled the blade Vezrath gave him from the sheath strapped to his back.

"Did he tell you what purpose the weapon has?" Dorin asked, and Lucien raised his brow at his youngest brother.

"Last I checked, a blade of this size was for taking off heads."

"No shit, asshole. You know what I meant."

"It is made of steel forged by Vezrath himself and embedded with the dust of a blood crystal from his realm. Only the king may carry it, and it is deadly to any fae. Royal or not," Amber replied.

"So, I cannot carry it?" Dorin asked.

Amber grinned. "Try it." She gave Lucien a look that said let their brother find out for himself. He held it out for Dorin to take and the second he laid his palm on the hilt, he jerked back with a yelp and shook his hand.

"Fuck!"

Amber laughed. "King only." She went back to sorting items in her backpack.

"Damn, that hurt like a son of a bitch." Dorin tried blowing on his hand as if that might help the large welt that had appeared there.

Lucien shrugged. "Well, now you have your answer." He turned back to Amber. "Tell us what to expect when we arrive."

"We are going to come in a mile outside the closest village. We can grab a few horses and ride closer to the palace under the cover of darkness. There is one guard station as we get closer. You'll have to kill the fae there or they will sound the alarm."

"I'd much prefer to jump straight to the king's chambers and kill him in his bed."

"He has guards outside his room. The man is paranoid." She faced him, her backpack strapped on and ready to go. "Don't forget, he is a royal and just as powerful as all of you. Maybe more so since he's been a royal since he was born and knows how to wield his power. He took down my grandfather and father. Do not underestimate him."

"Just lead the way." He linked with his brothers. *How are you guys feeling?* While he had been the only one that Vezrath had bestowed the full force of dark fae blood on, his brothers had gained a lot of their own dark power.

Ready to avenge our mother and sister. Both Andrei and Dorin assured.

Amber worked her magic. Her fingers pulling at the air in front of her. Her mouth moved, but whatever she spoke was so quiet he couldn't hear her words. A shimmer started right before a doorway opened and allowed them a peek at the other side. The moon was full and...

"Holy hell," Lucien whispered. "You have two moons." Simply looking upon them caused a burst of dark power to coil inside him like a snake ready to strike, and he wondered if his brothers felt it too.

Amber was the first to step through, followed by himself, then Dorin and Andrei brought up the rear. As soon as they were on the other side, the opening slammed shut. He took a deep breath, noting the air smelled of dark magic and black earth.

"Do you guys feel...different?" Andrei asked.

"Yeah. I have some damn dark urges, but I have it under control," Dorin replied. "Lucien? Your eyes have turned blue again."

"Here in Claromond, I can sense the light fae in both of you." She referred to Andrei and Dorin. "Try to cover it up." She looked up at Lucien. "There is no more light in you." Then she stepped into him and hugged him hard before taking a step back and giving a deep curtsey. "Welcome home, my King."

"Lead the way, Princess." Since they did not know where they were or where they were going, he and his brothers couldn't simply jump to another location. Amber was going to have to lead them through this realm.

"We can form a chain then I can take you to our next location where horses will wait for us. You'll need to hold hands." She reached for Lucien's while he took Dorin's and Dorin grabbed Andrei. As soon as they were all connected, Amber jumped them to a thick forest where there was a small clearing, and four horses were bridled and ready to bare mount. After each chose a steed, they followed Amber through the forest. Lucien had nothing to do but think, and in a moment of weakness he worried for his mate. Wondering how powerful he really was, he closed his eyes and let his horse follow the others while he searched for Elaina.

Seconds went by, but then there she was. As clear as if she stood before him and she was talking to Sonia. They were in Andrei's private office in the palace at Hetus, and also in the room stood Roman, Taos and Cristian. It relieved him to know the royal guards were with Elaina and Sonia. He desperately wanted to reach out to her but doing so was not wise. He had to keep all traces of her out of this war lest someone try to use her against him. Instead, he focused on Roman.

Roman, can you hear me? He watched his friend and noticed only his pupils dilated, giving nothing away to the untrained observer.

I hear you. Are you not in Claromond yet?

Yes. We are on horseback heading to our next destination.

Then how the fuck can I hear you in my head?

New powers. Don't tell anyone, Elaina will be upset if she knows, but I have to keep a distance between us.

I understand. Everyone has evacuated, and the women are discussing options. Sonia wants to stay here, but Elaina thinks we should move to the mortal realm. She is concerned about the queen.

Lucien smiled. His mate was a royal guard down to her soul. *I would agree, as I'm certain Andrei would as well. I will reach out later as we are closing in on our destination.* He severed his link as they approached the outskirts of a large village, and this was where his sister stopped.

"It will be faster if we go through the town's center rather than around. It's mostly shops that are closed anyway, so there shouldn't be any more than a couple of guards."

"Guards? In town?" Andrei questioned.

"Yes. The king has a curfew. We'll leave the horses here and make our way on foot and be sure you shroud yourself so no one can see you." She dismounted then removed her steed's bridle. "We will leave the gear over there by that tree and the horses will find their way back to their stable. Someone will collect this stuff after we leave."

"Why not simply leave the gear on them then?" Dorin asked as he dismounted.

"If the horses are spotted, they will simply think they escaped, but if they are seen with bridle, then an alarm will be raised."

"Good thinking," his brother replied.

Once everyone had dismounted and removed all the gear from their horse, they huddled together. "I think one of us should shift and fly over to check things out," Lucien said.

"Excellent idea," Andrei agreed.

"I will go, then I can keep all of you in my sight." Lucien wasted no time in shifting. His power sliding over him with an ease he'd never had before. Not that shifting was difficult, but this time it felt different, and he wondered if it was because the light fae was no longer fighting his darker side. It didn't matter. He flew out a few miles ahead of the others, so he could get a better view of any trouble his brothers and sister might run into. So far, the streets were quiet, and he didn't even spot a guard. He wanted to think they were having some good luck, but his gut told him otherwise. Something wasn't right about this situation. Amber had said there would be guards, but where were they? Just as he was going to fly down and ask her about it, all hell broke loose and an army of dark fae appeared from nowhere and surrounded his team. There was a small parting of the crowd that had their loaded bows pointed at his siblings, and a man wearing the gaudiest crown he had ever seen stepped through. Lucien thought about what to do. If he gave himself away, he would be useless to his family, so he made sure he remained cloaked and watched, thinking they would simply be taken prisoner and he could mount a rescue later.

He chastised himself, wondering how the hell they had walked into a trap so easily? One answer came to mind, and that was Amber's other uncle had sold them out.

"Well, well, if it isn't little Amber all grown and here to take the throne?" He laughed. "And you bring two light fae into my home thinking they can help you? Stupid girl." He waved his arm. "Kill them."

Arrows flew and before he could react, Andrei fell first, followed by Amber, then Dorin. Their bodies filled with arrows that he was certain held a poison fatal to fae.

"Leave them for everyone to see and know that their hopes of their princess coming to rescue them have been thwarted," the king commanded, and then one by one they all vanished.

Lucien hung on a current of air and let out a silent scream. Shifting, he dropped to his feet and went to Andrei first. No pulse. He checked Dorin and Amber, knowing he was going to find the same result. Falling to his hands and knees, he dug his fingers into the cold ground and let out a scream. His body shifted to his wolf under its own power and howled at the moons. It was the cry of a beast who had lost his pack.

Pain ripped through Elaina so fast it caused her to double over. Sweat beaded her forehead and had Roman not been walking next to her and grabbed her arm, she would have fallen to the floor.

"What is it?" he asked.

"I... Damn it, I don't know, but I feel like Lucien is in trouble. I know this isn't my pain." She looked up at the vampire. "Something went wrong," she whispered, thankful that the queen wasn't within earshot.

"Can you walk?"

"Yes." She straightened, and they headed further down the corridor when they heard a wailing scream. Not even looking at each other, they ran toward the heartbreaking cry and found Sonia in a heap on the floor, both Cristian and Taos standing over her, worry on their brows.

"He's dead," Sonia managed between sobs. "Andrei is dead. I felt him leave me only seconds ago."

Elaina and Roman looked at each other. "You need to get her out of here." She stepped closer to Roman. "I don't think Lucien is dead, but if his brother is gone, that might explain what I'm feeling."

He nodded. "The mating bond is complex, and you may indeed feel the loss of his brother."

"I need to find him."

He jacked a brow. "I should go with you."

She shook her head. "No. The queen needs to go to safety. I will do this on my own."

"How the fuck do you expect to slip into the dark fae realm?"

She glared at him. "I am not only a royal guard, I am the mate to the king of the dark fae. I will find him or die trying."

He closed his eyes for a second, then gave a curt nod. "I understand." He turned his attention to the queen. "Majesty, we must leave, now." He walked over and offered his hand and helped her to her feet. To Sonia's credit, she pulled herself together and looked at Elaina.

"You think Lucien lives?" Her voice was soft and broken.

"I do."

"Then bring him back to us." She walked toward Elaina with the determination of a woman who had a score to settle. "Bring my mate's body home, and I would also see the head of the bastard who took his life on a stake."

She tipped her head. "It would be my pleasure, Majesty. Stay safe." Then she jumped from the room to the outskirts of Hetus. Already dressed for battle in her black leather pants, boots and a black tank, she had a blade strapped to each thigh and one at her back. How was she going to get into Claromond?

"Lucien. Help me find you." She closed her eyes and pictured him. Allowed his pain to blanket her in misery. She saw a wolf, his wolf in her mind, and it howled the most agonizing cry she had ever heard. It took everything she had not to let the tears that wanted free to flow. There was no time for weakness. Her mate needed her and by the goddess she was going to find him. "Lucien, I'm coming." She imagined herself putting her arms around the wolf's neck and feeling his thick, soft fur between her fingers as she soothed the beast. Then suddenly, her body was pulled into a vortex and the next second she was standing beside the howling wolf.

She pulled the blade from her back and dropped into a fighting stance, her power at her fingertips as she studied her surroundings. On the ground lay the bodies of Andrei, Dorin and Amber, full of arrows, and she instantly knew they had been poisoned. She gazed up at the two full moons and felt a rush of power that was so dark and raw it nearly crushed her, but she kept her shit together.

"Lucien."

The wolf whined as it looked at her.

"I know, but we need to gather them up and get the hell out of here." The beast softened beneath her fingers and she knew that once again she had been the calm in his storm. His power ripped across her skin as he shifted, and the hard lines on his face showed his pain and determination.

He closed his eyes, tipped his head back and stretched his arms into the air, then shouted in a language that she had no idea what it was. Ancient fae? She was well versed in their language, but it was possible that the dark fae held one of their own.

A heavy black shadow covered the two moons, plunging them into darkness, and Elaina felt herself being pulled once more. Her body no longer under her control, she was sucked into some kind of vortex and the last thing she recalled was yelling out.

"Lucien, what the fuck!"

CHAPTER 17

His body trembled with despair, anger and a power so dark and ancient most wouldn't even know it existed. The words that fell from his lips, *"Bui i rod plural rodyn -o Vezrath, im lill i ithils na obeui nin conn-. Anand na- baw more a anand na- sab-."* By the power of Vezrath, I will the moons to obey my command. Time is no more, and time is mine.

The rip had been small, but it was all he needed and as he stood in the circle, he smiled at his success.

"What the fucking hell just happened?" Elaina's panicked voice came from beside him. Hmm, she shouldn't be here, but she was and so were the others and at this point he didn't give two shits.

"I bent time."

"Fucking Christ." She palmed her forehead, closed her eyes, then reopened them.

"Elaina, how did you get here?" Andrei asked.

"You... All of you were dead only seconds ago," she cried.

"Everyone be quiet, and I will explain." Lucien waved his hand through the air. "Amber's uncle led us into a trap. When we entered the edge of the village, the fae came from nowhere and hit you with poison arrows."

"What the hell?" Dorin scrubbed his head. "I don't feel dead."

"I called upon my powers and brought us back to this moment. Though I'm uncertain, why Elaina came with us, but I am thankful to have her here."

"Shit, I did not know you could do that," Andrei said.

"Me neither, but somehow I just knew."

"But that doesn't explain how Elaina even came to Claromond." Amber looked at her sister-in-law.

"I felt Lucien's suffering and was able to come to him." She looked at Andrei. "Sonia felt your death."

"Damn it." His face contorted in pain. "Hopefully, she feels this moment as well."

Lucien turned to his sister. "Why did the king think it was you coming back with two light fae to help you? He should have been looking for me as well."

"I let my uncle believe it was I who was coming to claim the throne. I told him I had two brothers who were going to help. The king does not know you exist."

"Why?"

"Because while a part of me wanted to believe Aven was helping, I had to consider he might turn on me."

"And you didn't think to inform us?" Lucien snapped.

"It was wrong of me not to." She looked at each of them. "I am sorry. This was all my fault."

"Even had we known, they may still have surprised us," Andrei said. "But you had four horses waiting for us, did he not question that?"

Amber shook her head. "I told him one was for supplies."

"We can discuss what happened later, but right now we need another plan, and it involves you three going back to join the others," Lucien announced.

"What do you intend to do?" Amber asked.

"Kill the king."

"What about me?" his mate asked as she shifted closer to him. He pulled her to his side.

"You will fight with me. You have earned that right."

"I'm not leaving." Dorin was the first to protest.

"Me neither." Andrei followed up.

"This is not your battle, and I have already lost you once. I'm not sure I can reverse time again, so please go." He left Elaina and walked to his eldest brother. "This is what you would do in my place."

"Prick. You know damn well it is. Fine, but I demand you stay alive and contact me the second that bastard is dead." Then Andrei pulled him into a quick hug, slapping him on the back before he released him and walked to Elaina. "Watch his back."

"Always," she replied.

"Let us take our leave. Lucien has this," Andrei said. "Besides, I need to see my mate."

"We can walk back a way and open the veil to the mortal world." Amber grinned. "Since you bent time and our attack has yet to happen, the king will detect it and perhaps think we changed our mind." Before she took her first step, power ripped a hole in the air and Vezrath stepped through it.

"I will claim my due now," the demon god spoke.

"What due?" Lucien's heart raced with panic.

"The price you must pay for my power. Do you think it was you who bent time?" He laughed. "It was I you called upon and I fulfilled your request, now I will take your mate as payment."

"Like hell you will." He pulled his blade, the one Vezrath had given him. "There was no deal made. You planted that knowledge in my head but conveniently left out the details of a trade." His fangs thickened, ready to tear flesh.

"It is not my problem that you do not understand the rules. Perhaps next time you will consider your options." He looked at Lucien's siblings. "You have three lives and I only ask for one. It is a more than fair trade."

"I will not give the life of my mate."

"I do not ask for her life. Only for her to serve me. You may bargain for her at a later time. Once you have your throne."

Elaina stepped forward. "I will go."

"No!"

"Lucien, you have another destiny to fulfill here."

"I cannot let you go." The pain that filled him was even worse than what he had experienced moments ago when he lost his entire family.

"I will go in her place."

Everyone looked at Amber.

"Vezrath, I am more valuable than she is. Take me and I will serve you until we can strike a bargain."

The demon grinned. "A princess, yes, I think you hold more value. I accept."

"Amber, no, you can't do this." Lucien was supposed to save his sister, not condemn her again. She moved into him and kissed his cheek.

"You need your mate, and our people need you. This is the wise choice." She looked behind her at the demon. "I will not come to harm in Vezrath's care but must stay until my mate makes a sacrifice to get me back."

"Your mate?" Andrei asked. "I did not know you had a mate."

"We are not bonded, but I sensed him when I was in your world." She stepped back and stood next to Vezrath. "For our people." Then she and the demon were gone.

"Who is her mate?" Elaina asked.

"No idea," Lucien replied as he tried to tamp down his anger. This was what the Falock had been trying to warn him about earlier. "Once again, our sister has been let down by her own family."

"Then do not let her sacrifice go to waste." Elaina touched his arm. "Take back your throne, then we can work at getting her back."

"She is right," Dorin offered. "Andrei and I will make sure word is spread of her fate. Hopefully, her mate will come forward and know what to do."

Lucien gave a nod then watched his brothers walk away, that heavy feeling back on his shoulders. "Did I choose the right path? I feel like no matter which one I walk on, someone has to pay a price."

"I'm so sorry, but I am here by your side. Together we will walk that path and deal with whatever lies at the end." Elaina wrapped her arms around his neck and kissed him, once again bringing peace to his tortured soul.

"I am happy to see you." He pressed his forehead to hers. "I don't know what I would have done had he taken you from me."

"You would have carried on with your mission, then you would have come for me."

He smiled. "I would have ripped Hell apart looking for you."

"I know." Her brows dipped in worry. "Would the king not have felt the power you used back there?"

"If he did, he would not have known what it was. He does not hold Vezrath's power because he does not hold the crown."

"How did he not kill you this last time?"

"I shifted to my falcon and hovered over the events in a cloak where none could see or detect me."

"Impressive. So, what is your plan?"

He grinned. "You and I are going to walk right into their trap."

"Come again?" Her eyes widened.

"Fear not." He looked up at the two moons. "Dawn is coming, so we need to go now while I can still draw power from the two moons."

"Are you sure about this?"

"Trust me." Everything inside him said this was the right choice. Once the fae here saw him and his power, they would turn on their current king and that would weaken the fae king, giving Lucien an even bigger upper hand. "Ready to make a grand entrance?"

She leaned in and kissed him. Fast and hard, it was full of Elaina and her passion. When she pulled away, she smiled. "I am ready."

He cupped her cheek. "I heard your words when I left."

She seemed relieved. "I am grateful for that. I'm only sorry I didn't tell you before you left."

He smiled and took a step back. Bringing his hand to the top of his head, he waved it downward over his body and changed his attire. The crown sat firmly on his head. Covering his chest was a silver breastplate with a falcon painted on the front, and the blade Vezrath had given him was strapped to his side.

Elaina gasped. "Damn you look sexy."

"Hold that thought for later." He held out his hand and when she slipped her smaller one into his, he jumped them to the center of the village. That alone was going to throw the bastard king off. He pulled the blade from its sheath and called out.

"I am your rightful king. Come and lay your eyes on me and see that I bear the crown." He held the blade to the sky where a bolt of blue lightning struck the tip and sent an indigo glow down the steel, encasing the blade and him in a soft glow.

Elaina stared in awe at her mate. Everything about him changed. His eyes went from cold, hard blue to near black, and even his face became more angular as his fangs extended. Immediately she sensed fae peering from windows and some even coming out of the shadows. Many of them appeared thin, as if they hadn't enough to eat. Before she could make further judgment, several warriors surrounded them and then the wrongful king appeared, two large fae flanking him.

He clapped his hands. "What a wonderful show. I don't know who you are, or how you came to have my crown, but I will have it back. Now kill them," he shouted, and his warriors raised their bows.

Before Elaina could react to the situation, Lucien drove the tip of his blade into the ground at his feet and the arrows bounced off an invisible shield that surrounded them. The faces of the fae warriors were one of shock, but their king's only held anger.

"Bring me that crown and the sword!" he snarled as he shoved the fae next to him forward.

Lucien lifted the blade over his head and swung it in a circle. With each arc, blue light raced outward and thrust the warriors off their feet until they flew back into the crowd that had now formed. Everyone gasped.

"You are going to die today, and I will release these people from your burden. For I am Lucien, the son of Princess Renna, her chosen heir to rule this world. You will pay for your crimes against my mother and my sister."

She looked around and saw fae dropping to their knees in mass numbers. Where had they all come from? When she looked back to Lucien, he glowed even brighter and the power that rolled off him was almost too much for her to stand against. There was so much darkness coming from him she knew her one and only duty was to keep him centered. To be his light in this world. She quietly found the link they held to each other and kept it tethered close to her heart. She allowed everything she felt for this man to pour through it. They had both come such a long way in a short time, yet nothing in her life had ever felt more right.

Her mate jumped and reappeared behind his enemy. The other fae was quick and in a flash had produced his own sword and spun to face Lucien. Steel clashed, and the sound echoed in the still air. Lucien pushed the king back with each step and swing forward. The king vanished, but Lucien looked unconcerned as his lids lowered and he dropped his head. She felt another rush of power course through her and knew her mate was using it to locate the coward who had vanished. As her breath caught, Lucien spun and met the sword that swung toward his neck. The impact of his own blade snapped the other in half.

She smiled as the king paled. Lucien gave no quarter to the fae now stepping back, panic rolling off him.

"For my mother and those she held dear," he yelled, and with one fluid swing, the fae's head was severed and landed several feet away. Lucien straightened and looked at the crowd that had gathered.

"Those who sold my mother into slavery and tried to kill my sister, you will face the same punishment. Run if you wish, but I will find you and end your miserable existence." His features softened as he relaxed and let the sword fall to his side.

"As for the rest of you, your life changes as of this moment. There will be no more oppression, but be warned, I will not tolerate war with the light fae." He looked at Elaina and held out his hand. "Your queen is light fae as well as my brothers, your princes, so it is time all of our people make their peace."

Everyone simply stared at him as if in disbelief of the events that had just unfolded. What had the former king done to these people? Finally, someone shouted from the crowd.

"Cheers to King Lucien, may the dark fae once more be a proud people."

The crowd erupted into more shouts and it was then the fae who was clearly the general of the previous regime stepped forward and dropped to his knees at Lucien's feet as he bowed his head, and on the verge of tears, he spoke.

"Thank the God Vezrath that you have come to save us."

CHAPTER 18

Lucien allowed the excess dark power he had pulled to him to drain away thanks to his mate. She really was the light in his darkness. After being led to the palace, they quickly took him to the throne where he currently sat, his mate next to him after someone procured and dusted off the queen's throne. Apparently, it had been moved to storage when the last king had taken over, as he wanted to be sole ruler.

What a selfish bastard.

Word had been sent to his brothers and they would be here shortly, but in the meantime, he had several matters that needed dealing with. The fae general had been a wealth of information. Regaling Lucien with the tales of torture and imprisonment bestowed upon those who refused to obey. The pictures the fae had painted were gruesome, and the first order Lucien gave was to release the stores of food that were in the palace to the outlying territories. The second was the removal of every trace of his illegal predecessor. Banners were ripped from walls and fae magic put to work, creating new ones for the falcon king since all had been previously burned. A new flag hung as well, showing all that Claromond was under new rule. That their ruler had come home. Lucien had also asked for three more thrones to be fashioned and delivered as quickly as possible. He'd tossed several gold pieces at the craftsmen for their quick work, and they were now installing them on the left side of Elaina's seat. He might be the chosen king of this realm, but the dark fae have two princes and a princess—once he figured out how to get her back—that had only the fae's best interest at heart. They would sit on this dais either with him or for him if he had to be away. However, he planned to do most of his ruling of Claromond right out there among the fae of this world. They needed to see him. To trust him and help him build a bridge between this world and that of the light fae.

He looked to his mate who was hotter than hell dressed in black skintight leather. Reaching for her hand, he whispered, "I hear the queen's crown is going to be spectacular." The previous king had stolen all the jewels and melted down the precious metals for his own use.

"I feel silly wearing such a thing."

"You'll get used to it. Especially when it's the only thing you wear in our bed."

She shot a heated glance at him. "I'm a king's guard, this will take getting used to."

"I'm certain Trevan will release you from your duties once he arrives here."

"He's coming here?" Her blue eyes widened.

"Yes. He and I will sign not only a peace treaty for all to see, but a trade agreement. We both felt it would be a crucial step in showing that we are friends and not enemies."

She smiled. "You are going to be an excellent king."

"And you will be a beloved queen of the dark fae."

"Those are big shoes to fill."

He held his hand out to stop the approach of the fae who was walking down the carpet. "Later, I will make up for my harshness with you before I left by making love to you all night."

Her eyes filled with passion. "I look forward to it."

Then he turned and gave a nod to the fae who continued forward. It was going to be a long day but knowing that his mate was by his side and in his bed tonight gave him all the strength he required.

"Your Majesty." The fae bowed. "Your guests have arrived, and we have prepared a brunch for all of you in the garden."

"Thank you." He rose and led Elaina off the dais and out of the throne room, grateful she was finally going to get fed. Her hunger had not gone unnoticed, and he chastised himself for not having seen to her sooner. When they reached the garden and he witnessed some of the people he loved most, sitting and talking. Some even laughing. Relief swept over him. It had been only hours ago that his siblings lay dead, and he had allowed darkness to overtake him so he could bend time and change the future. His brothers had left the seat between them empty in respect to their missing sister. Lucien ordered the flag lowered to half-staff and had given word of the sacrifice their princess had made on the fae's behalf.

He was tired. Weakened after the ordeal and needed to feed but would hold off until Elaina was nourished before he took from her. Taking a seat at the head of the table after settling his mate to his left, the servants delivered trays of food and drink. Everyone dug in and for a moment life felt normal again, except for the empty chair. Trevan who was at his right followed his gaze.

"I have my people spreading word of Amber's sacrifice. Her mate will come forward, I am certain of it."

"Thank you, but I worry he may not know of her existence. Is that possible among fae?"

"Fae sense their mates and while it is possible, he may not know who she is, I'm sure he sensed her the same as she did him. Perhaps he seeks a way to rescue her as we speak."

"I hope you are right."

They went back to eating in silence. Lucien picking at his food as what he really needed was blood. Elaina touched his mind.

Can't we go somewhere private where you can feed?
We have a brief reprieve before the treaty signing.
How short?
We have an hour.
That's all we need. Where are your quarters?

He stood. "Everyone, please continue to enjoy yourselves and we will join you for the signing." He offered his hand, then led his mate away from the crowd.

"Our room is being gutted, scrubbed and refurbished, but they have given us temporary quarters and it has a bed."

She offered a seductive grin. "Why, your Majesty, are you trying to seduce me?"

"Is it working?" He jumped them to the large, brightly lit room that held a king-size bed, and he didn't care what else. He removed his breastplate, hoping she might strip herself.

"It is, and since we only have an hour, can't you just flash our clothing away? I have no such power."

He cocked a brow. "Are you certain of that? You are my mate, after all."

Her gaze narrowed on him, and suddenly he was naked. "No fair. You're still dressed."

<hr />

She had done it! All she had to do was picture her mate naked, and it happened. Elaina was going to like this new power of hers but would have to remember not to think about such things when they were in public. It would be most embarrassing if their clothes suddenly vanished. She zapped her own away and lunged for Lucien. Time was ticking, and she needed him as badly as he did her.

He caught her and tossed her to the bed before he covered her body. "I promised you a session of soft lovemaking, but time is short."

"We have eternity for slow and soft. Right now, I just need to feel you." She gripped his shoulders. "I was so scared when I felt your pain. I had to find you no matter what." She placed a soft kiss on his lips before speaking again. "I don't know how to be a queen, but I know how to be a royal guard and Trevan has released me of my duties."

He pulled back to look at her. "What are you proposing?"

"That I be the first queen to guard her mate. Allow me to have your back. It's what I'm good at."

He grinned. "I can think of a few other things you're good at as well." He leaned down and sucked on her nipple, causing her to gasp and slip her fingers into his hair. Her mind was quickly falling under his spell, but this was important to her.

"I'm being serious."

He flicked this tongue, causing her nipple to become rock hard. "You can wear all the blades you wish under your gown. Have your clothing custom-made."

"Then you're giving me the job?"

He raised his head. "Whatever you desire, I will grant you as long as it makes you happy."

"It makes me very happy. Now, make me overjoyed by fucking me." She lifted her hips and ground against him.

"As you wish, my Queen." He gave her other breast attention while he slid his hand down her stomach and to the bundle of nerves that threatened to send her crashing headfirst into an orgasm the moment he touched her. His thumb circled her clit and when he sank his fangs into the swell of her breast, she shattered. Gave her mate the blood he required for life while he gave her release. Yet it was so much more than that. It was more than she could ever explain.

Sliding off her, he gave her a look of hungry, raw passion. "On your knees."

His command made her shiver. Lucien was the only one who ever saw her vulnerable side, and she loved that she could be herself with him. Rolling to her stomach, she raised to her hands and knees, spreading herself for him. He wasted no time in thrusting inside her. His thick length stretched her as he pushed inside and filled her. Everything fell back into place. They both were safe, and they were together.

His fingers dug into her hips as he took her hard and fast. She pushed back. Both of them held a desperate need. One that was borne of a deep hunger inside them. He reached around her and slid his fingers between her folds and across her clit.

"Lucien," she gasped.

He leaned over her and whispered in her ear. "You belong to me and I to you." Then he sank his fangs into her neck and pleasure burst across her body. The room tilted and faded as she screamed from the pure rapture he brought her. Lucien retracted his fangs and his release slammed into her. All his feelings opened up for her to share. His anger at his sister being taken, his relief that their mission had been a success and his siblings lived and then there was his love for her. So deep and pure it nearly made her cry. For once she dropped all her own barriers and let her feelings flow back to him.

Freeing himself, he rolled onto his back and pulled her to his side.

"People are waiting on us."

"I am king, let them wait." He rolled to face her. "I could not have gotten this far without you."

"I'm certain you would have done fine without me."

"I am blessed to have finally found you."

She smiled, her heart melting. "Are you sure about that? I can be one stubborn fae."

He laughed. "I would have you no other way."

"I love you." The words while still foreign to her felt right. She loved him and would freely admit he was a perfect fit.

"And I love you. How do you feel about living here?"

She didn't miss the fact he was concerned she might say no, but there was no way she could imagine living apart from him. Both of them were stepping into a way of life that neither had expected. "I will go wherever you are, and I would be honored to help build a bridge between the light and dark fae." She kissed the tip of his nose. "Now, let's get up before I have my way with you."

"I rather like the idea of you having your way," he growled.

"Later." She slapped at his groping hands, laughing as she scooted out of bed, and it was then she spotted the gown hanging on a door hook. "Where did this come from?" She moved closer.

"I believe that is a gift for the new queen to wear today."

"It's beautiful. Help me dress."

He let out a pitiful sigh. "I should keep you naked, and in my bedroom, but if you insist." He moved beside her, already dressed himself. She took in his black pants with black leather boots that reached up to his knees. His shirt was sleeveless, showcasing his falcon tattoo, the black material fitted across his broad chest. Over that he wore a sleeveless long coat of deep plum, and when he turned, she noticed the falcon crest on the back. With his crown atop his head,

Lucien looked every bit the dark king. She bit her lip, trying to rein in her desires.

Grabbing the dress, he held it open for her to step into, then went around her back and slowly zipped. His fingers lightly caressed her skin and sent shivers all over her body.

"You are beautiful, but there are a few items missing." He walked to the door, then opened it while she stared in the full-length mirror. The ivory gown had a sheer corset bodice covered in beaded lace appliques. The off-the-shoulder sleeves flowed to the floor with the skirt of layers of pleated lace. She felt like a princess.

When he walked back into the room, he carried a velvet pillow that held a crown studded with diamonds and five, very large, teardrop, dark amethysts.

"Another gift for the queen." He placed it on her head, then smiled. "Perfection."

She turned to look in the mirror once more and had to remind herself this was real. "Please introduce me to the fae who crafted the dress and crown so I may thank them."

"Of course, but I have one more thing. A gift from me."

She faced him. "From you? What is it?"

He reached into a pocket and pulled out the most beautiful ring she had ever seen. A teardrop amethyst crowned with five small round amethyst stones in a gold band. He took her left hand and placed the ring on her finger. "This stone is crafted from my magic. My love for you."

She blinked back tears. "It's beautiful. Thank you." Then she stepped into him and kissed him. Poured everything she felt in this moment into her kiss before she backed away. "We better go. Everyone is waiting."

CHAPTER 19

Lucien sat at the table that had been set up on the front lawn of the palace and where a crowd now gathered. Around him were the royalty from Drudora, Hetus and Glenmoore, as well as fae they had brought with them. They passed the official documents that had been drawn up stating the borders between light fae territories and Claromond would be open for all to travel freely. In addition, they had established a trade agreement between the fae that included not only food, but textiles and other valuable items. There were many talented fae on both sides, and this would help the sales of those items and hopefully start an internship between their people.

Once the documents had been signed and sealed, the party began. There were colorful tents erected all over the lawn, and music filled the air. Lucien stood with his brothers and looked on, watching as the light of day faded and the moons filled the sky. He wondered if the power he experienced flowing through him would always come with the moons rising.

"I wish Amber was here to see this," Andrei said beside him.

"I did not know my actions would lead to her being taken."

A warm hand touched his arm. "She took my place and I owe her a great deal," Elaina softly spoke.

"Trevan says her mate has come forward but doesn't wish to be identified yet." Dorin stood next to Andrei and watched a few female fae with an interested eye. Lucien chuckled to himself. It wasn't long ago when he would have joined his younger brother with his own roaming eye, but now all he could think about was Elaina. He cast a glance at her next to him in her new gown. She was a beautiful queen, and he'd already heard whispers of admiration from several dark fae.

"Did Trevan indicate when this mate of our sister's might come forward? Does he have any plan on how to get Amber back?" He would ask the king himself, but Trevan was walking the grounds with Storm and socializing with the fae. It was something he should do as well. He owed it to the people here to make himself as available as possible. Tensions still ran high for many, as was understandable. The dark fae had lived for several centuries under repression. They would not build trust overnight.

"He did not, but I say we give him a couple of days then we press him," Andrei replied as his mate walked up to them.

"Elaina, I would love it if you came with me to visit the tents." Sonia smiled. "I have a pocket full of Andrei's gold pieces ready to be spent."

"I think that is a wonderful idea." She gave Lucien a quick peck on his cheek, lifted her dress and walked off with her new sister-in-law.

"So, Dorin will be next to find his mate." Andrei jabbed his brother in the ribs.

"Not a chance. I'm not ready to settle down just yet, but when I do, I hope to be as lucky as you two have been."

Lucien let out a laugh. "Then you best go mingle. There are several females who seem to have their eye on the new prince."

Dorin didn't even reply but strode away with his chest out and head high, causing both brothers to laugh.

"He will soon be brought to his knees, just like you and I." Andrei faced him. "I am proud of you and what you have done here. I'm also relieved that our secret is finally out in the open."

"Agreed. Though I never expected this would become my role."

"Being king? You filled my shoes just fine."

Lucien shook his head. "A role I never wanted. I thought I lost you then and when you died in front of me this last time..."

Andrei put his hand on Lucien's shoulder. "I would have done the same, and the fact that our sister stepped in for your mate tells me she would have too. This was important to her, and at least now she can know that her people are free. We will get her back if we have to go after her ourselves."

Lucien only nodded. "Do you suppose mother would be proud of this?"

"I would like to think so. I wish we had been given a chance to know her better."

"As do I. Perhaps there are fae here who remember her." He looked at Andrei. "I plan to have a monument built in her memory."

"I love the idea."

Lucien brought his focus back to the crowd. He could still see Elaina and Sonia walking to the tents and stopping to speak to every fae they encountered. For once in his life, everything felt complete. He and Elaina had a big job ahead of them, but he was up for it. He had his brothers, his sister-in-law, and now his mate. The only thing missing was Amber, and his heart told him she would be home soon. His gaze fell to the man who would be her rescuer. It would seem he had gained the gift of vision himself. Yes, he knew Amber's mate and he would honor the man's wish to remain secret. There was also no doubt in his mind that Vezrath was about to meet his own hell.

ABOUT THE AUTHOR

Award winning and bestselling author Valerie Twombly grew up watching Dark Shadows over her mother's shoulder, and from there, her love of the fanged creatures blossomed. Today, Valerie has decided to take her darker, sensual side and put it to paper. When she is not busy creating a world full of steamy, hot men and strong, seductive women, she juggles her time between a full-time job, hubby and her dog, in Northern IL. Valerie is a member of Romance Writers of America and Fantasy, Futuristic and Paranormal Romance Writers.

Sign up for Valerie's newsletter and be the first to hear about new releases, receive special excerpts and exclusive contests. https://valerietwombly.com/subscribe

Follow Valerie
www.valerietwombly.com

- facebook.com/OfficialValerieTwombly
- twitter.com/fangedfantasy
- instagram.com/valerietwomblyauthor
- bookbub.com/authors/valerie-twombly

ALSO BY VALERIE TWOMBLY

More books you may love, visit my website to view all my books.

Eternally Mated Series

Guardians Series

Sparks Of Desire Series

A Jinn's Seduction Series

Beyond The Mist Series

Demonic Desires Series

Dark Horizons Series

www.ingramcontent.com/pod-product-compliance
Lightning Source LLC
LaVergne TN
LVHW091555060526
838200LV00036B/855